Pakul

GUILLERMO F PORRO III

Interior and Cover Build by Infinity Flower Publishing, LLC
www.infinityflowerpublishing.com

INFINITY

ISBN 978-1-0880-5899-2 (Paperback)

In dedication to my dad, Guillermo II, and my son, Guillermo IV.

Remember to always raise the bar from one generation to the next.

Chapter 1

When you think of a rabbit, you probably think of the white, puffy-tail-thing that hops around in the grass. Well, you are very wrong, because those are just the ones we use to spy on humanity. However, this is totally getting off the subject.

This is the story of how my life turned into a legend; one that causes grasshoppers to talk about how a tiny rabbit overcame all to become a hero. But, that was long ago, because right now I'm nothing more than a washed-up hero. I have been in exile for what feels like forever since I accidentally stewed a rabbit that was past his prime, which is against the law. So here I sit, on the edge of my porch as the rain clouds begin to flood the ground around my home. The rain just adds to my sadness, which is the reason my fur originally turned purple in the first place. Yes, I said purple—my fur was originally green, however due to the events that transpired, I changed colors. Well, that is simply enough of my rambling; let me go ahead and tell you my story.

My name is Pakul, and I was a simple little rabbit whose fur was as green as the grass on the other side. My family lived in a Carrotminium, which resides within the town along with some of the animals in this field. My older brother, Lio, is the rebel of the bunch but yet is still good at heart, even if he has the charm of a turnip. My sisters are Tess and Rose, who are completely different in their personalities, with Rose as the good one while Tess is the brains of the family. We all make things work inside of our house thanks to our parents. We live a normal life, which consists of eating carrots, hopping around the grassy patches of land, and occasionally dodging the Predators.

The Predators are a gang of foxes whose leader is an evil red fox known as Señor Saucy; rumor has it he is from the dangerous southlands. Our town has a wall made up of overly radiated carrots which protects us from anything or anyone who may try to invade. Like this one time when the Moles of the North decided to go in search of new soil. But that was before my time.

One morning, I opened my eyes to find myself once again on the floor as I did on occasions. While most of the time it is because I have slid off my bed, other times I have night-hopped off my bed. As I looked around the orange house, I found my sisters and parents in the kitchen. My parents were chunking up something onto some plates, while my sisters hopped up and down, unsure of what we were having.

"It's probably carrots like usual," I said as I stretched my fur completely out. My parents quickly spit out the last bit as they turned to me.

"Well look who finally decided to wake up," said my mom.

"Yeah, we almost got worried about you," Dad added with a slight smirk. Just before I could reply, my parents quickly placed two bowls of chunked carrots and lettuce in front of us.

"Oh, look at us! We're having lettuce today," I said as I grabbed hold of a lettuce leaf that slipped out of one of the bowls.

"Yep, mom went all out today," said a voice by the door.

We all turned to the front door where we found my brother Lio, whose brown fur was darker thanks to what I believed was mud. Of course, knowing my brother, what appeared to be mud could have been who knows what else. As he slowly hopped his way inside, we watched as he began to leave tracks of muddy footprints along the floor. Mom's eyes watered as his dirty prints soured the floor she had just finished cleaning.

"Great, now look at what you have done, mister. My feet soak up mud like a sponge!" my dad said to him. I could only laugh as my brother stopped, silent as his eyes lowered to see the muddy mess he had left.

"Well, thanks to you I have to buy more of that Caju cleaner," Mom whimpered as tears began to drop into the bowls of food.

"I just hope that this won't be hard to get off," Lio replied as he lifted up one of his large brown feet.

"It's ok Mom, I'm pretty sure Lio wouldn't mind at all spending his day to help you clean," I laughed.

"Oh yeah? Let's see how you like it," replied Lio as he balled up some mud and then chucked it in my direction. As the mud made its way towards me, it dripped all over as it dropped.

"Ha-ha, you missed," I chuckled.

"Oh yeah? Look again," he replied as I quickly began to look at my fur to check for mud. I found it right there in the middle of my green furry stomach, like I had spilled some of mom's brown sauce on me. As my anger began to take over, I looked over at Lio, who stood there laughing.

"You look like a field of grass that has a giant mud pie in the middle," said Tess as she finished swallowing a piece of carrot.

"Yeah, he does," agreed my other sister, Rose.

Their smiles widened as the mud began to loosen and then plopped to the floor. I quickly looked at my mom, whose face had reddened more as the amount of mud increased on her clean floor. In disgust, I quickly wiped off the rest of the mud while my family continued their laughter. As my mom stood there angrily, our dad quickly pushed us outside onto the doorstep and closed the door in our faces.

"I was going to say sorry, but then you had to open your big mouth," Lio said as he kicked me off the step. Before I could respond my dad's greenish head poked out of the window on the side of the house.

"Just go out and give your mom some time to blow off some steam," he said as his head quickly vanished back into the house.

"So how do you plan to clean this off?" I asked as I looked at the bits of mud on my stomach.

"Well that, my ignorant brother, is simple," Lio replied as he began to hop over to the pond behind our house. I could do nothing but shake my head and follow as he stopped on the edge of the pond. Just as I got there, he suddenly hopped straight off the ground and crashed onto the surface of the pond. In awe, I watched as he stepped out of the pond, the brownish color he had before getting muddy.

"What about me?" I asked him as he shook his fur dry.

"You're clean," he replied simply as I looked down to find the bits of mud gone from my fur. As we stood outside of the house, our ears could catch our mom still yelling inside of the house.

"How did we raise them to be such animals?" she yelled.

We quickly hopped up to the back window where all we could see was Dad shaking his head as he followed behind her. As we made our way back to the front of the house, we could still hear Mom venting inside through the half-cracked window. My dad's head appeared again as he watched the lawn ants begin to pack up their stuff and leave our yard.

"Sorry Mom, but just remember this was all Lio's fault," I said aloud as he me pushed out of the yard towards the road.

My dad's head went back inside as we quickly hopped our way towards the town square. The town square was the area in our town that the locals would go to for business. As we began to hop closer to the bustling market area, some of Lio's friends appeared from the crowd. My brother had a usual group of misfit friends whom he liked to hang around with that most of the time got him in trouble. It was also quite apparent that their reputation was known, due to the different traders watching them carefully as they passed. The three then made their way out of the crowd as they approached with a grassy bag that TC was holding in his claw.

"What were you able to grab hold of today, TC?" asked my brother as the mantis dropped the bag in the center of our little group. TC was my brother's nickname for this praying mantis that he had known since he was my age.

Of course, from the stories my mom told me, they were getting into trouble even at that early age.

"Nothing really special, just the usual grubs and vegetables that can be easily grabbed," TC replied. Just as he finished, Briann scurried in between the two of them.

"Hey, Deputy Lio, what do you think of this?" asked Briann as she pulled out a shiny shell from a pocket she had made in her fur.

"Deputy Lio?" I replied with laughter before my brother shoved me.

"Yeah, it's because you know I'm skilled like that," my brother replied as he puffed out his chest.

"So what do you think of my beeswax shell?" she asked again.

"It's nice," he replied as he searched the bag before his eyes suddenly widened.

I could never understand how my brother could be so dumb to the fact that Briann had a crush on him. Briann was the newbie of the group who had only been taken in because she was a lone hamster in a world of field critters. They loved the fact that she was able to escape from her cage and had survived an attack by a dive-bombing hawk. She was one tough cookie, with a scar upon one of her cheeks from the hawk fight. As she dropped the shell on the floor, Lio pulled a crisp new carrot out from the bag, putting a smile onto TC's face.

"Man, you've got some good eyes to find that in a bag full of stuff," TC said.

"They don't just call me deputy Lio for nothing," he replied as he held the carrot in front of his gleaming eyes. As my brother was about to shove the carrot into his mouth, he stopped and quickly hid it when he remembered we were still there.

"Let's not forget that the funniest comilean in the world is here too," says Trippe.

"What in the world is a comilean?" I asked as I watched his eyes twitch in circles. Suddenly all eyes were on me.

"You tell him, Trippe," said my brother as he tried to keep from looking down at the carrot.

"I am half comedian and half chameleon, or that's what my nametag said before I took it off," Trippe said.

"Yeah, however his jokes are really poorly timed," said Briann as she nibbled on a pellet she pulled out of the bag.

"It's not my fault no one can appreciate good humor nowadays," Trippe replied as he turned his back to Briann.

"We appreciate you," said TC.

"Oh yea? So what do a pig and a hamster have in common?" asked Trippe.

The gang looked at one another confused as Trippe stood there with a smirk.

"What?" asked Lio.

"Your both such bores," said Trippe as he began to laugh hysterically. Briann's brownish fur began to redden.

"Alright you two, chill out before I pinch you somewhere painful," said TC as Briann stared at Trippe.

"He does have a slight advantage over you," I said as I turned towards Briann.

"And what's that?" she asked me while she looked up at Trippe.

Trippe's eyes twitched as he suddenly launched his tongue into the air, grabbing a moth that tried to sneak past. Trippe began to smirk as he chomped down upon the moth, and Briann looked on nauseated.

"Just think, I'm not even fully grown yet. Soon I will be a mega comilean," Trippe laughed.

"That's good. Hopefully that will kill your dreams of doing stand-up," said Lio.

As we bickered back and forth, the crowd in the marketplace lessened as the day began to fade to night. Suddenly we stopped, as the towers began to ring that danger was approaching. Our eyes widened as we quickly began to run off towards the door of the General Carrot. We ran inside and quickly shut the door, the bells suddenly stopping as a rumbling began just outside the carrot walls.

"Who is it?" I asked innocently as I stared out the window.

"Wow, just how stupid can you be," replied Lio as he placed his head down into his hand in frustration.

"It's the Predators and that dastardly sly Señor Saucy," the shop rabbit said as suddenly a group of foxes appeared in the town.

There were five of them as they rode in on rabbits that they had captured from our very city. They were a mean bunch, especially their leader who rode in the front with one hand holding a rope which he dragged on the floor. The rope was in the case any of us rabbits decided to grow some pellets and attack him or his group. His groupies were oddities for sure, especially Char, who was the group's muscle.

"Some say he was found inside of a laboratory covered in chemicals," says Briann as her fur shivered against the window frame. Everyone in the store gulped as the group rode past the shop and continued towards the farm section of the town.

"Where are they going?" I asked aloud as the group continued to watch them ride away.

"No idea, but rumor has it they are in search of Master Tarroc," replied the shop rabbit.

"I guess that makes him quite a catch," said Trippe as everyone turned to him, shaking their heads in disgust.

"That was your worst pun yet," said TC, who usually ignored what Trippe spat out. As we stood in silence, the bells in the guard tower rang, announcing that the predators had left our town and things were again safe. We all exhaled gently as Briann snuck outside to make sure the coast was clear. After she had made it to the road with no harm, we one by one walked out of the store and headed back to the marketplace.

"So who is this Tarroc fellow?" I asked.

"Hare legend states he can use carrots as weapons," my brother said as he looked around for the bag.

"What you looking for, Deputy?" asked TC as he stared at my brother who had begun to stare at the road.

"The bag has gone missing," my brother replied. He then looked down at his sash to find his carrot safely tucked inside, to his relief. Before we could speak another word, suddenly I spotted my dad as he hopped his way towards us from the direction of our house. My brother and I quickly hopped out of the way as he pulled up, sweat dripping from his furry forehead.

"Hey Pops, how's it going?" my brother asked as my dad's buckteeth showed, which was usually a sign of anger.

"Where in this carrot-crunching world have you guys been?" he yelled as Lio and I dropped our heads.

"We've been here," said my brother as TC and the others began to walk back towards the market.

That was usually how things worked; when one got in trouble the others usually left it for dead. Which is ok, because even I shuffled a bit away from my brother who was dead in my dad's sights.

"Go home now!" my dad yelled as he shifted his ear towards the direction of the house. As my brother made his way towards the house, he kept his head down the entire way to avoid making eye contact. Our dad watched as he walked down the alley towards our house before he suddenly turned his attention on me. My eyes quickly darted to the reddish sky.

"Why do you follow in his hops?" he asked.

"He is my brother, and I don't do everything he does," I replied as I lowered my eyes for a quick second. My dad's teeth disappeared beneath his top lip fuzz as he calmed down.

"Well, just don't get into the trouble he has gotten into," he replied as he hopped closer to me. I nodded my head as he approached my shoulder and placed an ear upon it.

"I guess it is late," I said as I began to walk down the alley. My dad hopped behind me to make sure I did not stray from the path or try any funny business.

As we hopped past all the empty roads, we hopped through the dusk into the beginnings of the night. Finally, just as the moon settled in the sky, we arrived home. We quickly approached our walkway, where Mom stood in the doorway with her arms folded.

"She looks upset," I said as I turned to my dad who nodded in agreement.

"Yeah, I wonder if your brother has dealt with her wrath," he replied.

"I truly hope so," I replied just as my foot landed upon the massive lettuce leaf we used for a walkway. As we continued down it, suddenly a confused look came across my mom's face.

"Where is Lio?" she asked as we arrived.

"I sent him home first and watched him hop himself towards the house," Dad replied as he began to grow angry.

"He was the one I told you to make sure came straight home. This is the good son," she replied, motioning to me.

"I'm here!" a voice yelled out which caused us to turn towards the road in front of the house. As we all looked, my brother hopped quickly over to the opening in the fence that led to our walkway. He hopped himself in between my dad and I in order to dodge Mom's stare. Of course, the fact that he was taller than I was certainly did not help him trying to hide from her.

"Where did you go?" Mom asked as her arms tightened around her chest.

"I took the scenic route home," he replied as he quickly dropped his head to the floor.

"I'm not playing, we were worried sick about you," she replied.

"I know, but I did hear a funny joke thanks to Trippe, whom I saw on the way here," he replied as he raised his head a bit.

"So try it on us and dig yourself out of this trouble," my dad replied as he pushed him in between her and us.

"Ok well, what do you get when you combine a rash and a vegetable?" said my brother. We all thought about it for a second and then shrugged as we gave up on trying figuring it out.

"What is it?" I asked as he began to smile.

"Radishes," he said as he began to laugh, his foot thumping the ground. He suddenly stopped as he watched us not even break a smirk, the whistling of crickets filling the air.

"Hey Mr. Darny," I said to our neighbor who waved back as he whistled himself back into his house.

"Please just get back in the house, troublemaker," my mom said to my brother. All he could do was keep his head lowered as he slowly made his way past Mom's bushy tail. As I tried to follow him inside, she placed her arm in the doorway and blocked me.

"Where do you think you're going, little one?" my dad asked.

"Inside to bed," I replied as I stepped back.

"You can, but first we just want to make sure that you're not getting yourself into any trouble," Mom replied as I looked at her.

"We thank our lucky feet that we at least got one good son," my dad replied.

"Don't worry, I don't think that will happen," I replied as she moved her arm and allowed me to enter the house.

Once inside the house, I found my siblings stretched out upon their beds as mine lay vacant, awaiting me. As I hopped over to my bed and placed my tail gently on it, I watched my parents come inside. I quickly laid back and shut my eyes as my parents went to their room and closed their door. As I let out a deep breathe, I found my sight to go from dark to suddenly a massive explosion of light.

Chapter 2

As I opened my eyes, I found myself on my bed, which usually meant it was not a bad night. I rolled to the side of my bed and sat on the edge as I wondered what awaited me in the other room. I opened the door and found nothing; no action, not even a whisper coming from my parent's room

"Where is everyone?" I said aloud as I walked past all the empty beds.

I continued my search when finally I noticed some shadows coming from outside of the window. I grabbed a step stool from the table and placed it by the window so I could step on top of it. I looked out and found my family standing alongside the fence with their eyes focused down the road. I quickly hopped off the stool and headed for the door, realizing that not just my family was outside, but the entire town was out by their fences. They were all looking in the direction of the great carrot wall and the entrance of the town. As I slowly made my way out the door, I watched as suddenly the Rabbit Force came down the road.

"Hey, Stan, we could use your help," said the leader of the Force as my dad hopped out of the driveway. My dad followed the group down the street as they headed past my line of sight.

"What's everyone looking at?" I asked, as I got closer to the rest of my family along the fence.

"That," replied Lio as he reached out his hand to point to the wall. To my shock, the carrot wall that had stood through everything was on the ground leaving our town vulnerable.

"How could this happen?" my mom asked aloud.

"No clue but the rumor is that Saucy and his gang had a part in this," said the shop rabbit who was dragging a bag on the floor.

"Those sly foxes have nothing better to do than try and torment us," Lio replied.

The shop rabbit nodded as he continued down the road and towards the Force, which was examining the wall. As we watched on, the Force began to spread out as my dad stood back and they attempted to lift the wall. Just as they had gotten the wall to just above their head, suddenly the massive carrots broke in half. As the carrots crashed back to the earth, despair and sadness consumed the entire town. We watched in horror as the carrot pieces crunched on the ground.

The force quickly regrouped in front of the broken shards as the town watched in silence. After some brief moments, the group broke off and began to clean up as my dad began to hop back towards us. When he finally got to us, all he could do was hop past us silently, with droopy eyes as he hopped back into the house. My mom quickly hopped into the doorway to console him.

"We will make it through this," my mom said as she rubbed his back.

"I have never witnessed such a horrible event in all my days," he replied as he stared at the blank wall.

We stood outside, we watching as the Force began to remove the wall in pieces and send them to sink inside of Lake Harrbit. Once the last piece was gone, the Force then went one by one to all the houses to make sure they answered all questions. When they arrived at our yard, we all stood behind the fence as we tried to gather up the courage to ask. Even Lio could not muster anything as the Force just stood there. Finally, after a few awkward seconds, my parents reappeared from inside the house to talk to the gentlerabbits.

"Do we know how it happened?" asked my mom.

"Indeed we do, it appears to be the Predators," replied Captain Barr as the rest nodded their heads.

"So what is the next move?" asked my dad as he made his way towards the group.

"Well, we are simply unable to do much besides bide are time and re-build," replied Captain Barr.

Finally, my brother had enough and swallowed his weakness as he stood at the fence. "So what you are saying is they are going to get away with that," Lio stated as he pointed at the black space where the wall would have been.

The group looked at one another with frowns as they turned back to him and nodded. Something inside my brother snapped at that moment. His eyes began to redden and his mouth began to clench as the rest of us watched on, unsure of what to do. My brother quickly turned back to the house and hopped so great that he made it to the house in one hop. Unsure, my parents looked on from the fence as my sisters hopped towards the outside window. I hopped inside the house to find my brother by his bedside.

"What are you going to do?" I asked as my brother began to peel back some of the carrot skins underneath his bed. I watched his eyes widen as he pulled two sharpened carrots out from the ground below. He then placed them in his side fur as he placed the carrot skins back into their place.

"I'm going to teach those vermin a lesson in rabbit warfare," he replied as he began to make his way to the door.

"Then I'm coming with you," I told him as I grabbed some carrots from the counter.

"Don't be foolish, bro, you need to stay here," he replied.

Of course, I wouldn't listen; he could never go at anything alone. I mean, they had defiled the town in which I was born and I was not going to let them get away with it. He hopped out of the door as I stood there in silence as I watched him hop over the fence and past our parents.

"Aren't you going to stop him?" asked Captain Barr.

"One thing about Lio is that once he has decided something, you don't stand in his way," my dad said as my mom began to cry. My sisters quickly comforted her as my dad stood there in silence along with the captain.

Back inside, I tried to figure out a way to follow him without anyone seeing me. I realized the back window was just large enough to allow for a small rabbit like myself the ability to escape unnoticed. I made my way over to the window and leaped up just high enough to grab hold of the window frame. I managed to pull myself up and then squeezed my fur through the window as I dropped to the ground. Before I hopped away, I turned back to sneak a peek to see that everyone was still in the front.

I then turned away from the house and began to hop towards the outside of the town. As I hopped around the edge of the town, I spotted my brother hopping on the road outside of town that headed to the Predator's hangout, also known at Tortabbi. I was sure that was where he was going and I knew he was going to need some backup. Honestly, as I stalked my brother, I kind of felt like a fox, following him for the last mile. Just as I was about to move in, I suddenly saw three lights just down the road from where my brother was.

They appeared to be flames of some sort, but I was not sure because before I got a good look they disappeared. As I continued, I began to worry if my brother had seen the lights too. Just as I moved my eyes away, I fell into a pool of murky water that made me lose track of him. To this day, I can still feel the disgusting muck against my fur as I struggled to swim to the surface. I quickly made my way to the moonlight as I breached the water's surface where I found clean air.

With my lungs filled with a fresh breath, I made my way towards the shallow part of the pool. Stepping on the muddy grass, I quickly moved to my feet in order to locate my brother. I found him just in front of me, directly in front of three shadowy figures, which I could not make out, in the dim moonlight. I squinted as I noticed that two of the figures were much taller than the third and one of them happened to look somewhat like TC. Then it hit me, the group of shadows had to be Lio's buds that snuck out to meet him out of the town. It was obvious as the clouds moved, revealing Trippe's twitchy eyes.

"Here, this should help you," said TC, whose claws shown bright green in the night air.

"Yep, you should definitely be able to outfox those foxes now," said Trippe as he spit out his tongue and grabbed a nearby firefly. I tried to avoid being sick as he crunched down on it. A tiny shadow jumped onto Trippe's head.

"Don't forget to grab the real prize," said Briann as they looked towards a misshapen carrot that was lying on the ground.

"What is this?" asked my brother as he leaned over and picked it up.

"That, my deputatious rabbit friend, is a rabbit pellet gun," said Trippe with a silly grin.

"You know that he is going to fight foxes, right?" said TC as he looked over to Trippe.

"Yeah, I know, but come on, it's a weapon and a snack whenever he is running low on food," replied Trippe.

"But still, why did you choose pellets?" asked my brother as he held the gun to his eye level.

"Because only rabbits eat those things," replied Trippe as Briann stared down at him.

"Wow, you are not only a bad comedian, but you're stupid too," said Briann as she jumped up and down upon Trippe's head.

"Didn't you know hamsters eat them, too?" said my brother.

"Yeah, but what is the possibility that he would have another hamster encounter?" replied TC as he turned towards Briann.

"I'm just saying, who knows what kind of criminal mind a hamster can have," replied Briann as she moved her hands to the top of her head.

"Oh please, what's the worst thing you can do? Cause someone to sneeze?" replied TC as a smile came up on his serious face.

Briann quickly folded her arms as my brother placed the gun into a grassy holster along his furry waist. As my eyes bounced back and forth, I completely ignored the sounds of the grass in front of me breaking. This was not smart, seeing as a second later it broke, which sent me falling forward and into everyone's view. Their eyes widened as they realized that I had thrown a rabbit into their plans. As I watched on from the ground, their faces had grown red with anger as they began to think about how I could complicate matters. I was sure the last thing they thought would happen would be for Lio's innocent little brother to just pop out of the grass like a weed.

"How long have you been there?" asked Lio as he broke the awkward silence. I quickly looked around at the group.

"I was there long enough to hear about your plan to get revenge," I replied as I quickly got to my feet.

My brother nodded his head with a frown as he began to whisper to his friends. Then suddenly, Lio turned back to me with a smirk and a large stick in his hand. Before I could respond, he tossed the stick in my direction. As I reached my hand out to grab it, I managed to grasp hold of the last bit that stopped it from hitting the ground. I looked at the stick and then turned to my brother, who just stood there with a smirk upon his face.

"I'm surprised he caught that," said TC.

"Don't worry, I'm shocked myself 'because he has no coordination at all," replied my brother.

"I'm not that bad," I said as I suddenly slipped upon a dirt clump landing back in the dirt.

My brother and his friends simultaneously released a laugh that I am sure could be heard back in our town. As I picked myself off the ground, their laughs quickly quieted.

"Okay, well then, come on Pakul, let's go and bring your stick with you," replied my brother as he hoisted the bag above his shoulder.

I nodded my head, holding the stick in my mouth as I hopped over to him. Once I had passed him, he began to follow me down the road towards our destination.

"You guys be careful," said Briann.

As we sped up our hops towards Tortabbi, we passed quietly beneath the stars. We never looked back to see how far we had gotten. While the moon made its way through the cloudy night, we found ourselves having to stop suddenly as we came upon a fork in the path. While I looked down the identical paths unsure, my brother shook his head and continued down the path to our right.

"How are you so sure?" I asked him as he looked back at me.

"This isn't my first sneak-out, muddy," Lio replied as he continued to hop down the path.

I quickly began to hop after him, my ears twitching in irritation. I mean, really? Had he never fallen like I had or done something that was a misstep? As I caught up and then overtook him, I quickly looked back at him struggling to keep up his speed.

"That's what you get for eating all those carrots before a run," I laughed as he looked back angrily.

Before I could turn around and watch where I was going, suddenly the road turned away from the current direction. Unable to stop, my speed sent me off the road and tail-first into a field of mud. After I landed and the pain in my tail had faded, I opened my eyes, feeling the shield of mud on my face.

I quickly lowered my ears and cleared off my eyes to see the large plot of mud where I had landed. From left to right, all I could see was brown and clumpy, until finally I looked behind me at the moon-lit green hill from where I had fallen. At the very top of the hill was my brother, who was looking on with the largest grin a rabbit's mouth could have held up.

"You are such a hare," laughed my brother as I tried to pick myself out of the mud.

After managing to clean myself a bit, my eyes widened as I realized the stick had disappeared from my mouth. I quickly looked all over for it when suddenly my brother let out a cough, which caused me to look back at him.

"What is it, chunky?" I asked.

"You looking for this?" he asked as he tossed something into the air that I could barely see in the light of the moon. Before I could pick it up in the sky, it suddenly hit me in between my ears and then dropped in front of my feet.

"Ouch that hurt!" I yelped as I bent down to grab hold of the stick.

"Dude, it's called coordination. You should work on it," he replied with a chuckle.

"Whatever. How do I get back up to where you are?" I asked as I began to examine the hill in front of me.

"That's easy, just put one foot in front of the other," he said.

I shook my head as I managed my way up the hill towards the road. As I slowly made my way to the top of the hill, the sky above me cleared to allow the moon light to shine brighter than it had the entire night. Finally, I made it to the top as my brother looked on with a grin. I looked down as well to find myself looking like a brown and green ladybug.

"Whoever called it mud should have called it disgusting," I said as I tried to clear the spots from my once bright green fur.

"Look, just 'because you don't have a lucky foot doesn't mean you can go and hurt the mud's feelings," my brother said.

"Ha ha, rabbit's foot. Not funny," I replied as I threw a ball of mud at the back of his head. The mud smacked his brown fur.

"That was uncalled for," he said as he began to spin in a circle, trying to see where he'd been hit. He finally gave up and hopped over to a shrub that was reflective from the moonlight bouncing off the dew dripping off it. He saw the brown patch that was darker than his own brown fur and he shrugged, placing his back up against the shrub to wipe the mud from his fur. As he pulled away, he looked back again and then turned towards me as I stood there on the path.

"Are you ready yet?" I asked him as I began to hop down the path. I continued down the path and after a bit found my brother hopping right behind me once again with a gleam in his eyes.

Honestly, I was somewhat scared that if he had caught me that he would have knocked me back down. I quickly hopped away from the muddy field and headed towards the smoke-covered section of sky. As we continued to hop closer to the town, we found ourselves suddenly engulfed in a dense fog. I slowed in order to see through the fog, but my brother maintained his speed as if he was immune. He even managed to catch up as my eyes squinted just to focus on staying on the path.

"Hey, stop over there," he said as he pulled ahead a bit before he turned off by a crevice in the bushes. My eyes on alert, I followed him and stopped in front of him.

"Why did we stop?" I asked him, barely able to make out his brown fur through the fog.

"I just wanted to tell you to be careful and don't be too innocent in this town," he replied.

"Oh, please, what is the worst that can happen?" I scoffed.

"Believe me, you don't want to know," he replied as he began to hop down the path once again.

Just before my mind could explode with things that could happen, I followed behind him back onto the path. We slowly made our way out of the zone of fog into clearer air. The air in our lungs felt refreshing without us having to suck in the burnt fog. Then I spotted it on the horizon— Tortabbi, the city in which nightmares were born.

The very place's greenish glow erupted in the night sky like a volcano as its buildings broke the horizon. With our eyes focused on the town ahead of us, we kept pushing forward, even when the air in our lungs seemed lost. My brother suddenly slowed down enough so I could catch up, and then he suddenly nudged me off the road.

"What are you doing?" I asked as I began to nudge him back.

"There is something coming," he replied as we skirted into the overgrown grass.

As we lay down, I looked over at my brother, whose eyes were focused on the road. His ears twitched as suddenly a vibration began to cause the rocks on the road to bounce up and down. Suddenly, a screech rattled the air, and in the distance appeared some sort of monstrous creature. It was gray and appeared to be some sort of box carrier. We stood still as it grew closer, along with the Predators leading the way still on rabbitback. As the group passed us by, we spotted the ropes that were tied to the creature, which was forcing it to keep up with the group. Then it passed us by, leaving us in total darkness as its massive frame blocked the moonlight. We continued to watch as they kept going out of our sight down the path towards the town.

"What in the world was that creature?" I asked as I began to creep back onto the road.

"That, my muddy little friend, was an armadillo, which is not very common in these parts," said my brother as he followed me onto the path. We found ourselves stepping down into one of the footprints left behind by that massive creature.

"How do you know what it is?" I asked as my brother began to hop towards the town.

"I have seen it once before, when it knocked down the walls of our town when we first put them up," replied my brother as I caught up to him.

"Wow, you've seen a lot in your old age," I said as I extended my hops into a longer stride that allowed me to catch him.

"Don't be funny, because if it wasn't for my age, you would have been trampled," he replied.

Before we realized it, we had gotten closer to the town than we expected. We quickly slowed our hops as we began to enter a much more dangerous part of the road. This part took us toward the entrance to Tortabbi, and was lined with broken down wagons, remnants of abandoned trade stations, and bones from those who had not survived. The ground began to get harder as our feet struck it and we kept our sight focused on the path ahead of us.

After a mile or two more, there it was in all of its corruptive beauty, right in front of our very eyes. It was surrounded by fields of dead soil and swamps that could lead to the demise of any creature, especially at night. We suddenly stopped as we watched the town begin to glow from the greenish lights within the center of the town.

"Is it too late to turn back?" I asked as my legs began to wobble and shiver.

"Oh, my little brother it was too late when they knocked down our wall," he replied as we began to hop underneath the lizard skeletons that lined the gateway.

Chapter 3

Shivers ran down my fur as we walked into the town with a sense of fear and nervousness. I managed to keep an eye on my brother as I examined the dark and gloomy town. The town's main road was filled with creepy and troublesome that was just waiting for you to slip up. My brother and I turned at a corner in order to get away from the sight of all the folks in the street. He then turned to me.

"Hey, do you remember what I told you?" he asked as my eyes jumped back to him.

"Of course, you said something about not looking so innocent," I replied as he suddenly took his nail and scratched my cheek. I quickly jumped back and held my hand upon my cut cheek.

"Are you crazy?" I yelled loudly which caused dragonflies above to explode off the rooftop. I removed my paw and found a little bit of blood squeezing from the cut as it rolled off my face.

"Now you fit in," he replied with a smirk. Before I could yell at him, he quickly hopped over to the main road to be the look out. I slowly hopped behind him and used my ear to slap the back of his head.

"That's my payback," I said as I peeked past his outstretched head. All I could see was the low-level trading that happened occasionally in the dead of night on the edge of our town, illuminated by the green glow.

"The glow is from these lights that provide a killer shock," Lio said as a dragonfly crashed to the street with a sizzle. The smell quickly nailed my nose, and I pressed a paw over my nose as we watched two flying insects remove the body. Before we could blink, the body was gone, and everyone returned to normal.

"I don't think I want to know what happened there," I whispered as Lio's eyes remained on the street.

"You're right, lost rabbit," said a mysterious voice followed by a loud cough.

My brother's eyes widened as he quickly turned and we both looked into the darkness to see where it came from. Just as our eyes began to focus upon the greenish tinted shadows, suddenly a creature stepped out with its body covered in a blanket made from an old napkin. As it got closer to the greenish light, we could see the pale wings that barely touched the garbage-covered ground.

"I have seen a lot in my years, but I have never seen a bug of your type," Lio said as the stranger stopped in his place.

"That's because I'm a bug of love, and cities can only handle so much loving," said the stranger as he let out another cough.

"I've read about you in Bug Weekly once," I said as my brother frowned and placed his paws over his face.

"My young friend, that is certainly something you don't want to admit in this town," said the lovebug as my brother smacked me in the head with his ear.

I rubbed the back of my head as I tried to keep my focus on the stranger and ignore my brother.

"Yeah, you are probably right on that," I replied.

"So stranger, what's your name?" asked my brother.

"It's Bugnova the lover, and yours are..?" he replied.

"My name is Lio, and that thing there is Pakul," he said.

"Ah well, if that isn't the sign of love in the brotherly way," chuckled Bugnova.

"That's not love, this is," I snapped as I quickly turned and shoved my brother down onto the grime-covered road.

Bugnova and I looked on with smirks as Lio picked himself up and wiped the dirt off his face. Before he could respond, the green lights suddenly dimmed, sending us into the dark. As the three of us slid along the wall, we managed to poke our heads around, spotting them.

There they were, standing alongside their rabbit prisoners in front of the armadillo. The dastardly, sly Señor Saucy walked towards the armadillo. He leaned over and opened up something that I couldn't make out in the darkness. All I could see was that he grabbed something as he quickly walked back over to the rest of the Predators. When he got back, they began to chuckle as they all walked together to a massive rock. Suddenly, one of the members lifted the rock and, one by one, they jumped in as they disappeared into the darkness.

"Where are they going?" I asked as we watched the last of them jump in before the rock closed behind. There was no response, so Lio and I looked back to find that Bugnova had disappeared from sight.

"Bugnova?" yelled my brother, but there was no answer.

We both shrugged as we turned back, just as the lights above returned to their regular level. My brother looked at me and nodded as he hopped back into the faintly lit road. I took a deep breath and hopped after him, just as the rest of the undertraders began to reappear. As we hopped toward the armadillo, we were forced to stop in our tracks when the rock lifted up.

Startled, we glanced around for a good hiding place, settling behind the armadillo, whose eyes were closed shut. We moved as close to it as we could without waking it.

Just as our hearts began to race, the shadows of two figures appeared, along with the sound of crackling laughter. While my brother watched the shadows, I stared around, suddenly spotting a shard of glass across the street. It was reflecting everything that was going on, including us huddling next to the armadillo. I continued to watch, as the foxes grew more detailed and they grasped hold of the rabbit slaves. The rabbits were led underneath the rock, disappearing from view. Once they were gone, Saucy and another member remained just outside of the rock.

"They will love the carrot bath they are going to receive," laughed one of them, who I presumed was Saucy because the other just simply agreed.

After a few seconds, they both went out of view as the rock quickly dropped onto the ground. As my brother and I regained our breath, we quickly hopped towards the front of the armadillo. We then looked around to make sure the coast was clear as we looked back at the rock front of us.

"How can you hurt someone with a carrot?" I asked Lio.

"I don't know, nor do I really want to find out," he replied as the armadillo exhaled, which caused us both to jump.

As I tried to regain my wits, Lio slowly hopped to the rock, being as silent as he could. I watched as he examined the rock and then crouched down to look at the bottom of it. I quietly made my way over as he suddenly rose up and then lifted the rock. It revealed a decline toward a tunnel, which was lighted better than the town was. Lio looked at me and then turned back towards the entrance. Just as he was about to lift his leg, something cleared its throat. Our eyes widened as we looked around, spotting the armadillo.

"You won't be lucky if you put your feet into that hole," it said.

"Why is that?" my brother replied as he inched closer.

"You foolish rabbit, the only things that survive down there are tough and sly," it replied.

"I am those things," my brother stated.

"What about him?" the armadillo asked, motioning to me.

"He'll be fine. I'm sly enough for both of us," Lio replied as he flexed his rabbit arms.

"You're not just foolish…oh well, don't say I didn't warn you," replied the armadillo as it shut its eyes once again.

Lio looked satisfied as he looked at me. "Here little one, you should really put this on," he said as he reached into his pocket and pulled out a dark, dyed hat.

"What is this for?" I asked as I grabbed the hat from his hands.

"To give you some sort of tough look," he replied as he placed the rabbit pellet gun he received in its place.

I shook my head in annoyance as I placed the hat onto my head with a bit of a lean. My brother smirked before quickly looking back to the tunnel entrance. I watched as his chest swelled as he hopped under the rock and out of my sight.

"Here goes," I said aloud as I hopped slowly behind him down the dim ramp.

I quickly found my brother just in front of me as he figured out what he was going to do. His face tightened as he proceeded through the tunnel, lit by beeswax candles. Ahead of us was a plastic lid which someone had turned into a door, rimmed by a light on the other side. It seemed like time stopped as we hopped closer to the door without making any sort of noise. After we closed the distance between the door and us, we both looked at each other.

"You better be ready for this," whispered Lio.

"I think I am," I replied as my brother reached out for the makeshift door handle. He then twisted it and opened the lid, allowing the light behind it to escape into the tunnel. We found ourselves in what appeared to be a different world beneath the city. We stood in the doorway, in awe of what we had just discovered.

"What is this place?" asked Lio as he slowly crept forward.

"You're asking me," I replied as I struggled to take in all that I was seeing. I had never seen anything as complex as what I was seeing at this moment. Before I could take in anymore, Lio turned back and pushed me behind some barrels that were standing at my side. Before I could question his motives, he quickly placed his furry ear in front of my mouth as he nudged his head to the left. My eyes wandered over where I spotted two beetles, who were walking in our direction. As we pressed tightly against the barrels, they walked past us and through the doorway that we'd just entered through. Just as they closed the lid, Lio removed his ear and hopped away from the barrels to make sure things are safe.

"Wow, Saucy has some impressive helpers," Lio said as he looked around.

Once again, before I could respond, my brother took off down the path, leaving me behind the barrels. I quickly bolted out and silently followed him as we passed numerous crevices along the dirt walls. We suddenly stopped as we passed one that had an orange light that pulsed from out of the shadows. My brother turned to me and then looked back toward the crevice as he gingerly made his way over. I watched as he took a deep breath and then lifted one of his brown feet and placed on the muddy floor of the crevice. He then placed his other brown foot inside and disappeared from view. After a couple of seconds, my heart stopped when I realized that I was very alone with who-knows-what possibly lying around the corner.

"Oh, why me?" I whispered as my green feet were frozen to the ground.

"'Cause it's funny to watch your green fur turn yellow," said a familiar voice. I watched as my brother's brown head appeared from the crevice with a massive grin.

"You would be scared too, if it wasn't for that little gun of yours," I replied as I hopped towards the crevice.

"Oh, please, I'm such a bigger rabbit without this," said my brother.

I quickly approached the crevice as my brother made room inside so I could join him. After I was safely between the dirt walls, I followed him towards the orange glow that had attracted us to the crevice. As we made our way deeper, the walls began to widen, which allowed us more room to breathe as we watched the orange glow grow brighter. We stopped when we found ourselves at the end of the crevice. It had led us into a place unfamiliar to us, which contained numerous figures. We looked on as the shadows gathered up as one of them began to drag one of the rabbits from earlier towards the group. The rabbit's eyes widened as it is pushed closer to the edge when suddenly one of the figures stepped into the light of the room.

"It's Saucy," whispered my brother as he kept his focus upon the room ahead.

"How can you tell?" I asked as I snuck a peek past his shoulders, finally seeing whom he was talking about.

"He's the only fox I've seen with a scar like that over his eye," he replied as Señor Saucy's arm rose up into the air.

Our breathing slowed as suddenly his arm dropped as the rest of his gang began to laugh menacingly. We then watched as the red rabbit suddenly turned blue just before the fox pushed it off the edge. The Predators stood around as suddenly an orange liquid rose over their heads and then quickly dropped back down.

"That rabbit is definitely stewed," said Señor Saucy aloud with a chuckle.

The rest of the gang began to laugh hysterically. Just as he stopped laughing the rest of the gang stopped as well, which returned the place to almost total silence. He then raised his arm once again, as one of the members went out of our sight, to the pleasure of his grinning leader. I looked down at my brother, realizing he was shaking and breathing heavily with rage. His hand, which was on the gun, tightened as the member reappeared with another slave rabbit in tow. The member then dragged it to the edge and was about to push it over and I shut my eyes to avoid watching its demise.

"Stay here, no matter what," said my brother as a bang popped through the air. I quickly knelt down and watched in horror as my brother approached the remaining members of the gang. The slave rabbit stood frozen with its eyes wide in shock as the gang's eyes reddened with anger.

"What are you doing here?" asked the leader as the rest of the gang stood in silence.

"I'm here to make you pay for what you have done to my town," replied my brother as he raised the gun upward. The leader's eyes sank downward as he watched the gun reach his level.

"I'm getting out of here," said the slave rabbit behind my brother as it turned around away from the action. Just as the rabbit began to walk away, it suddenly stopped, an evil grin on its face. My eyes widened as the rabbit's tail suddenly enlarged and its face grew more fox-like.

"It's a fox in rabbit clothing!" I yelled, which caught everyone by surprise.

Just as the leader was going to respond the white fox rammed Lio in the back, which sent him crashing into the shoulder of the leader. Two of the members grabbed hold of him as Saucy quickly knocked the gun over the edge into the orange liquid. As a bit of courage rushed through my blood, I hopped from out of the crevice into the light with my stick in hand.

"Oh, look what we have here. It seems like a rabbit fiesta," said Señor Saucy as my breathing quickened. He stepped in between my brother and I as my brother continued to struggle to break loose.

"Let me go, you rabies-infested, wolf-wannabes!" yelled my brother as he struggled.

"Will one of you shut him up?" Saucy replied as he began to scratch at his eye patch. The white fox snuck behind my brother and placed his hands over my brother's mouth, which muffled the sounds.

"Is that better, Señor?" asked the fox.

"Mucho, thank you," replied the leader as he stared at me, the stick still grasped in my hands.

"You better let him go," I said as my chest began to swell.

"Si, I will. Tomas y Brenton, let's get rid of him," said Saucy as the two foxes began to drag my brother towards the edge of the cliff. I charged at Saucy with my stick raised high above my head as I swung it at his head. Just as the stick was about to strike him, one of the members sped in between us and took the strike across his head. We then watched as the fox stumbled over to the edge and lost his balance. As the rest of the gang watched, the orange liquid exploded upward, and Señor Saucy stood face-to-face with me.

"Fantastico. I could have used him in my plans," said Señor as he shook his head.

"This one is for you," I replied as I quickly raised the stick up and sliced it at his head.

This time, before I could strike him, he snatched it out of the air and then threw it into the air above the orange liquid. My jaw dropped as I stepped back, uncertain of what else I could do. A dastardly smirk came to his face as the rest of the gang looked on with teeth-filled smiles. Señor Saucy turned to the side, looking between my brother and me as he debated what to do. He scratched his foxy chin, then suddenly turned to my brother and gave him a massive shove, which sent Lio flying off the cliff. Tears began to roll down my face as I tried to run and save him, only to be held back by the two foxes that had just let him go. It was torturous and haunts me today, the sight of my brother's face as he fell into the liquid. He crashed down, sending a wave of liquid up into the air just as the foxes began to move me closer to their leader.

"Now, what to do with this pathetic hare?" wondered Señor Saucy.

"I say we let him join in the same bath as his brother," replied the one I believed to be Tomas. My eyes reddened with anger as I tried to break free from their hold. Saucy suddenly grabbed a hold of my neck and dragged me over to the edge of the cliff. Just before I got to the edge, he stopped and then grabbed my head as it hung over the orange liquid.

"I hope your little rabbit nose remembers that smell," said Señor Saucy as I took some of the smell through my nose. "That's the smell of roasted rabbit."

"You're a monster!" I screamed out as I tried to wriggle free.

"Me a monster? No, rabbit, I am nothing but a fox," he replied with a chuckle.

"Señor, shall we add more carrot juice to the pit?" asked one of the foxes behind me.

"I think we shall, just so we can stew his brother even more," Saucy replied as he picked me up to watch as the two foxes dropped gallons of carrot juice into the hole.

My eyes watered as I watched them, the hot carrot juice roiling. I felt my fur shake, and I stood helpless, unable to do anything to stop them from doing any more damage. Then as if my ears had broken, everything went silent around me. I felt Saucy loosened his hold and he turned me around to face the other foxes. To my surprise, they were standing there with their eyes bugged out, just staring at me.

"Looks like we have here a purple rabbit!" yelled the leader as the rest of the gang began to laugh. As the tears dripped down my face, I looked at my feet and found purple instead of green.

"How did you change colors?" asked the leader as he re-tightened his grasp.

"I don't know!" I cried out as I tried to understand what was happening. Before I could think on it, Saucy pushed me into the arms of two of his gang members who held onto me tightly. They turned me around so I was forced to look at their leader.

"Fellow Predators, what we have here is a special breed of rabbit," said Señor Saucy as he began to pace the floor.

"How so?" asked of the followers. The leader then stopped in mid-step as he turned his head toward the fox who had just spoken. Before he said a word, one of the other foxes slapped him in the back.

"Stupido, we all know rabbit come in all colors, however a special few change colors when they suffer changes in emotions," replied the leader. Señor Saucy then stepped toward me with an evil grin upon his foxy face.

"What are you going to do to me?" I asked as my legs began to wobble.

"Not him, but us," said one of the two foxes that were holding my arms as they suddenly began to push me forward.

I struggled to break loose, suddenly I felt myself being sent over the edge of the cliff. I screamed as I saw nothing but the vast pool of the steamy carrot juice below. My eyes shut as I prepared to crash to my demise, when I stopped suddenly and began to be pulled upward. My heart was pounding in my chest and I was frozen, fixated on the juice, when a pair of furry hands grabbed hold of my ankle. The hands then pulled me back, and hope of being saved from this predicament filled my head. However, I was instantly sent into despair when I spotted the fox's faces.

"Darn, it didn't work. Oh well," said Saucy as he and the rest of the foxes began to laugh. As my breathing began to recover, I looked down at my foot, where I found a rope attached.

"You aren't sly, you're just mean!" I yelled, causing the smiles to fall from their faces.

"That was mean," said Saucy as he shoved me back-first off the edge.

My eyes shot downward as I felt myself go feet over ears, towards the juice. Just before I shut my eyes, I spotted the other end of the rope falling with me. I shut my eyes as I lost all feeling and I approached my juicy demise.

Chapter 4

My eyes reopened and I found myself face-first on grassy ground underneath a blue sky. I closed my eyes and then quickly re-opened them to make sure I was not imagining where I was. I then quickly turned onto my back as I enjoyed the fresh air and bright sunshine. With my furry tail on the ground, I slowly began to get up as I tried to figure out what had just happened.

"Did I dream all that?" I asked myself aloud as the breeze whipped through the long grass.

As I began to get to my feet, my mind flooded with all that I had experienced. I quickly grabbed my head as my eyes shut as I tried to shake the images away. My eyes then re-opened into the grassy field, and I suddenly realized that my arms were purple. I quickly examined my entire body to find that all of it had turned to purple. I pushed my feelings down and looked around me.

I found nothing but grassy fields, so I decided to go through a wall of these overgrown shrubs that stood in front of me. While I pushed my way through, I tried to avoid the sharp thorns and bits of human trash that had been caught up inside the shrubs. I then finally cleared my fur from the shrubs and safely placed my feet back onto the ground. My eyes widened, as ahead of me laid the shattered remains of the place I called home. I hopped quickly towards the town, thinking about who I was going to tell about my ordeal, and better yet, what happened to my family. My eyes watered as I approached the town as I thought about all the things that could be waiting for me.

"Come on Pakul stay strong," I told myself as I continued down the road.

As I looked to the left and right, all I saw was grass covered in dirt, as if something came and sped through. I suddenly found myself slowing down when I spotted the indented footprints of rabbit tracks. They appeared larger than my own and were in long running strides. As my memory began to jog, I remembered that I had seen these prints once before inside of Tortabbi, just before we went underground.

As my eyes followed the tracks, they aimed straight for the town. With a renewed strength, I hopped off to town as quickly as I could. The prints suddenly multiplied into three different sets, all heading the same way. I quickly looked up when I realized that I was merely feet from the very road that I had set off from what felt like a day ago. The air stood frozen inside my lungs as I made my way inside the gates, looking at the destruction. However, before I could walk any further, I found myself before two sneering foxes.

"Welcome to Saucy Square," said one of the fox guards as he extended his celery stalk into my face.

"Saucy Square? What happened to Hareville?" I asked as I looked around the ruin. The two foxes turned to another and began to laugh a foxy chuckle.

"That's so rich. Hareville, what a pathetic name," said the other guard as he leaned upon his celery stalk.

"Yeah, I mean, no wonder Master S was able to destroy this place with ease," the other replied.

"No… it can't be… and what of the citizens of this town?" I asked which appeared to anger the two foxes.

"That's easy, you pest, they were captured and enslaved into our Foxholes," replied the guard as he placed his celery back onto the ground.

"You vermin, how dare you!" I screamed as I took off past them and ran inside of the town with hopes of finding some sort of sign.

"Finally, some kind of action," said the fox as he threw down his celery and began to chase me down.

As he ran after me, all I heard was a crack from the celery and then a thud of the other as it smacked into the floor. I hauled my tail through the town as I looked around for some sort of way to hide from this fox. I then looked back briefly to see that he was a few feet away. Then I made a regretful decision by making a left, which left me face-to-face with a dead end. I was instantly frozen in my tracks by the ruins of a house that had blocked my last escape plan. As I stood in front of the house, the fox's shadow cast over me.

"Now what am I going to do?" I whispered as I continued to check around the street for any sort of item that could help. As my eyes shot around, I saw a post with radishes that were tied around it.

"Let's just mark this population down another notch," said the fox as he began to charge at me.

Before the fear could overtake me, I quickly slid over to the post and managed to lift it up into my mouth. With the taste of radishes filling my mouth, I quickly swung my head, which sent the post crashing into the fox's head. The fox grimaced for a second before it turned around angrily, its jaws clenched.

I quickly spit out the post, letting it land into my furry paw where I held it tightly. The fox then suddenly jumped but before it could hit me, I flung an end of the post in between its eyes. The fox fell to the ground, unconscious, which allowed me to regain my breathing. After I checked to make sure it was down, my eyes wandered to the exit of the alley that was now clear of any foxes. I placed the post back into my mouth and I hopped away from the fallen fox. As I arrived at the empty road, I found no sign of the other fox, instead hearing a crash behind me. I then turned around to find the other fox knelt down next to the fallen one as it stared angrily at me.

"By your lucky rabbit's foot, you are going down," it said as it suddenly took off after me.

I headed towards the exit on the other side of the town—only to find the carrots that had once built our walls were now keeping me from a clean getaway. As I approached the large carrot, suddenly pain filled my head as memories flooded me with all that had transpired. I was frozen in pain in front of the carrot, suddenly flung to the floor with a sharp claw at each of my sides. My face tightened from the pain, and the fox lifted me up just as the other had managed to hobble his way over. Unable to keep my eyes open and focused upon the foxes, I could barely make it out as it stood in front of me.

"I wonder what we should do with this pesky rodent," the fox said as the other held me from behind.

"I think we should remove it from sight, 'cause it will look bad with Master S that he got this far," the fox said.

I squinted as my head throbbed, watching the fox moving closer to me. It then quickly swiped at my face, which knocked the radish post from my mouth onto the ground. As the pain worsened in my head, the fox grabbed hold of the post and threw it into the air over the wall.

"I say we bring him to the Foxholes," the fox smiled as he turned around towards the town square.

"Yes Captain, be right there," the other fox chuckled as its grip suddenly loosened a bit.

My eyes suddenly exploded open as I threw my foot down upon his tiny foot. As he yelped in pain, I quickly hopped away out of the town as I tried to ignore the pain that had filled my head.

"It's ok, let the vermin go. He has nowhere to go out there," he said with a chuckle.

As I continued to hop away, the pain in my head vanished instantly as I realized he was right. Who will help a rabbit, or even more important, is there even anyone out there who is not a fox?

While my thoughts swirled, I watched as the heavy brush began to thin out until finally it shrank back to a normal length. The sky above appeared flushed with clouds as shadows increased the shade on the empty plains. I began to look around the field as I tried to figure out what I would do. Then unexpectedly, my thoughts suddenly flashed back to when the foxes had run through our city. They were looking for someone, if I had remembered correctly, someone by the name of Master Tarroc, my brother had said. The only problem is I had no clue where to find him or if he was still alive. Then, as if the great rabbit god had heard my thoughts, I spotted a sign just a mile down from me that appeared to be pointing in one direction.

"What can go wrong?" I said aloud as I continued to hop towards the sign.

As I grew closer to it, I found the road forked with one side leading to a pile of rocks while the other side was clear. I quickly looked up at the arrow, where some writing had been scribbled, which was pointed in the cleared direction. My eyes shifted back and forth and then I began to hop onto the clear path. After a few minutes of silence, the wind began to whip, making my fur tingle from the slight drizzle that had begun. I hurried my pace in order to avoid as much of the rain as I could. I tried to look for cover, and I spotted an old tree that sat upon the hill like a statue in the town square.

Just as I prepared for another massive hop, the ground gave way and sent me to the bottom of a shallow hole. As the pain in my head renewed, I tried to find my way out, realizing water was beginning to fill the hole. I quickly planted my foot on one of the sides, trying to push myself out of the hole. However, my foot lost grip and plunged me back into the rising water. With no other idea what to do, I let out a massive scream with hopes that a random creature would come and rescue me.

All I heard was the rain and the echo as it bounced off the empty fields that surrounded my location. As the rain crashed onto the top of my head and down my eyelids, I tried one last thing. I stepped towards one of the walls and found some soft soil hoping my buckteeth would be good for a different use.

I jammed my teeth into the soil trying to ignore the muddy taste. With my mouth against the wall, I placed my hands into the soil, and, to my surprise, I found myself successfully managing to creep up along the wall and out of the hole. Just as I had made it to the halfway point, suddenly a massive earthworm plopped onto my green nose. To my dismay, my nose tickled and as hard as I tried to fight it, I ended up letting out a sneeze that threw my backwards and back to the bottom of the pit. As the hopelessness set in, my tears began to drip down through the raindrops that had laid claim on my puffy cheeks. I got up from the dirt and once again tried to find a soft spot in the soil to place my teeth. After I had located a place near the original spot, I was about to insert my teeth, when lightning lit up the area and the wind quieted down a bit.

"You are going to hurt those by doing that," said a voice from out of nowhere.

I quickly pulled my teeth out and looked all around for the source of the voice when suddenly another flash of light revealed new shadows. My head turned upwards and I spotted two shadows of equal size standing at the top of the hole.

"What do you foxes care about me hurting my teeth?" I yelled out.

"Did he just call us foxes?" one of the shadows laughed.

"Yes TC, he did. I think we should leave him here," the other replied.

"Wait TC? Is that you?" I asked as the rain turned to a drizzle and the clouds began to allow some light to escape through. I spotted TC with his head covered in a grass hood, standing alongside another figure of equal size.

"Indeed, and this is Master Tarroc, who is definitely not a fox," replied TC as the other figure began to lower down his walking stick. My eyes widened as I reached out my hands and grabbed hold of it. They both slowly managed to lift me out of the hole and back onto solid ground. As I regained my footing, TC looked down at me with his claws down to his sides.

"I'm sorry to hear about Lio," said TC as he reached one of his claws out to get me back to my feet. As I reached out, my eyes widened as I wondered how he had exactly known about Lio.

"How do you know about what happened?" I asked him as brushed the mud off my face.

"That, young one, is a question I will answer once we get back to my safehouse," said Master Tarroc as he began to walk towards the tree that overlooked the plains. I nodded my head as I began to hop after him, until TC stopped me suddenly.

"I wouldn't step there unless you enjoy being at the bottom," he said as he moved me into the grass that lined the path. I nodded my head as he and I quickly followed behind Master Tarroc. We reached the tree just as Master Tarroc had entered the shadowy hollow within the bottom of the tree. We quickly followed behind him as TC pushed a large rock into the opening that allowed us inside. Just before the sun was sealed out, Master Tarroc walked over to the side of the tree and pulled slightly on a dusty rope. I watched as the rope triggered two massive fronds at the top to open, which allowed the sun inside. As the fronds stopped, my eyes turned toward Master Tarroc as he sat at a wooden table with TC at his side.

"So who told you about my brother?" I asked them as I pulled up a twig chair from underneath the table and sat down.

"Well, Master Tarroc informed me of how he came across you being tossed into an orange liquid," replied TC as he looked over at Master Tarroc.

"Indeed, I also mentioned about seeing a brown rabbit having crashed first and then a green one who had come to the rescue," said Master Tarroc as he raised his hand to scratch his rigid goatee.

"I just have one question for you," I replied as I faced Master Tarroc.

"Ask away, young one," Master Tarroc said as TC sat in silence.

"How did I get saved from my impending stewing?" I asked as TC's eyes bounced over to Master Tarroc's area of the table.

"As I watched you fall, I quickly threw down a magical blue carrot which teleported you out of danger," said Master Tarroc as suddenly the pain in my head re-intensified. It was so powerful that I reached for my head, tears once again flowing from my squinted eyes.

"What's wrong with him?" asked TC as he ran over to my side and placed a claw onto the fur on my back.

"I was afraid something like this would happen if I used the Aquarrot," said Master Tarroc as he walked around the table. My head then slowly rose up from the table, which allowed TC to back away in relief.

"What do you mean something like this?" I heard TC say as the pain subsided a bit.

"Yeah, what's wrong with me?" I asked as he turned towards a chair that leaned up against the tree.

"There is a side effect of an Aquarrot. It causes the user to have an irrational fear towards what they last thought of," replied Master Tarroc as he turned and sat upon the chair.

"So what was my last thought?" I replied as I tried to fix the fur on my head.

"Well, let's just say it's something us rabbits love so dearly," replied Master Tarroc as he began to slowly rock in his chair.

"You mean carrots," said TC, which instantly launched me into a flood of chaotic memories. My head then returned to the table as my eyes shut instantly as my thoughts clouded with a bright orange fog. After a few seconds, my eyes reopened to find TC and Master Tarroc watching me carefully.

"Yep that's definitely it," said Master Tarroc as TC frowned and covered his mouth with his green claws.

"Sorry," he mumbled from beneath his claws as I tried to shake the remnants of the pain.

"It's ok, I guess we know not to mention the C word in front of me," I said as I sat up straight once again. Master Tarroc sat back in his chair and then let out a little snicker as he closed his eyes.

"It's not that simple, you also can't see it either," said Master Tarroc.

"Well that might explain me shutting down in the town," I said as I began to get up from the table. My eyes zipped upward, toward the fading sunlight, which meant night would soon arrive. I then looked down at TC and Master Tarroc as they both continued to prepare for the upcoming day. TC was preparing a bed on the floor, for which he used the fall leaves and some remnants of a picnic from a while back. Master Tarroc just sat back in his chair as he gently rocked himself to sleep.

"You know, Pakul, there was still something I wondered about," mentioned TC as he continued with his preparation. I raised my hands to my face to see that TC was talking about my new purple fur that I slightly remembered changing.

"Well honestly, I don't remember much about that part of the night," I replied as I tossed some twigs at his feet.

"Sounds like a night me and your brother would have," he chuckled as he carefully gripped the twigs in his claws. I let out a chuckle as I walked over to the bed he was setting up, only to find he had finished. It was a simple thing that was not extremely high which used sticks for legs and a palm frond for a blanket.

"Cozy," I said as I slowly placed my tail upon the grassy mattress. TC shook his head and gave me a shove, which sent me onto the bed where it did not break.

"What, you were expecting it to break?" he asked as he began to walk over to other side of the trunk.

I replied with a smirk as I lay back on the marshmallow pillow as TC disappeared into the darkness of the trunk. I lay there, lost in my thoughts while Master Tarroc and TC took their places in the trunk to sleep. I shut my eyes but before I could fall asleep, my memories suddenly jarred me awake. My eyes then quickly widened as I found myself a spectator for the incident that sent me over towards the hot juice. I sat on the edge as I watched myself be thrown over with the rope attached to my ankle.

"NO!" I screamed when suddenly I watched as I disappeared into a cloud of blue smoke. I quickly looked all over the rim of the smokestack to search for Tarroc when I suddenly spotted a hooded figure on the other end. The figure looked up with green eyes as it suddenly disappeared, leaving me on the top alone. I quickly looked back down to see the foxes scrambled as they tried to figure out where I had gone. Then before I could make a move, my sight went black and I found myself in complete silence.

My eyes reopened to find myself back inside of the trunk as I faced the wall. As I laid there, unable to fall back to sleep, I tried to turn myself over, however I failed miserably. I guess someone forgot to tell me that rabbit do not have the proper spine to lie on their backs as I have been told humans can do. I grew angry, and finally exhaled as I launched my rabbit legs into the side that propelled me onto the floor. Apparently, when I landed, I actually was heavy enough to send some of the leaves to come down through the hole at the top. I watched as they landed all around the room including one on top of Master Tarroc's head. Of course, he was out so it just landed there as he sat there without even a flinch.

"That wasn't smart," I whispered to myself as I tried to calm down.

"No it was not," a voice replied in the room. I watched as Master Tarroc flicked the leaf from his head as his green eyes met mine.

"I'm sorry, I had a bad dream," I whispered as I tried not to wake up TC whom was still in the shadows.

"Bad dreams, you say? Well I have a cure for that," he replied as he tossed me an object which I could barely make out.

"What is this?" I asked as I raised the object into the moonlight.

"That, my friend, is a radish, which is very good for bad dreams," he replied as he tilted his head back against the wall. I remember thinking that this rabbit was crazy but oh well, and I took a quiet bite out of it. I then watched as it fell to the floor and my eyes began to shut and my mind began to go silent. I felt my legs give way, and I laid still at the foot of my bed.

Chapter 5

The next morning, my eyes opened to find the freshly lit sky over me as the sound of feet clattered on the floor. I stretched off the ground, which attracted the attention of TC and Master Tarroc who were about to exit the stump.

"Well look at who finally woke up," said TC as he cleared the hole, which allowed the light inside.

"TC, leave him alone. He is probably drowsy after taking a bite of radish," replied Master Tarroc as he poked TC in the back with his walking stick.

I smirked as I stood up, spotting the radish still on the floor next to me with a bite missing. I picked it up in my hand as bits fell to the ground from the part that I had bitten. As my face was lit up by the light from outside, I noticed neither TC nor Master Tarroc were visible, which left me alone in the trunk. I quickly hopped out into the light, spotting TC out in the field as he took apart stalks of grass. As my ears shielded my eyes from the sun, I made my way out of the trunk, feeling the sun beating down upon my head. I continued to watch TC as he made swift work of the batch of stalks he had in front of him. I spotted Master Tarroc sitting on the weedy soil underneath a peeled back piece of the trunk. He motioned me over to him so I hopped over into his shady spot.

"Morning Master, what is TC up too?" I asked as the gentle breeze whistled through the grassy hills around us.

"His training," he replied simply as TC suddenly jumped up and front flipped out of our sight.

"So what do I do?" I asked as I laid down upon the weeds.

Master Tarroc brushed his goatee and reached out his hand, the post that the fox had thrown appearing suddenly. My eyes widened as he examined the post before dropping it onto the floor and pointing to the ground. I bent down and grabbed the post with my hand, still in shock that he had found it. I pointed out into the hill, where suddenly TC reappeared with an acorn he had found.

"You must learn how to correctly use the radish for your fight," said Master Tarroc as TC stood up the pinecone on the floor.

With the post in my hand, I nodded my head and walked over to where the pinecone stood. I could sense TC as he stared at me, standing in front of the pinecone with the post drooped from my hand. I took a deep breath and tried to attack the pinecone with the post but it was caught between two rows of scales. I struggled to free the post from the scales and they fell to my feet, instantly freeing the post. I stared at the post as I wondered if I had dislodged it, only to have my hopes shot when I spotted TC smirking at me.

"I loosened it for you," I said as TC went back to cutting the stalks of grass. Suddenly, the post was jarred from my hands and I looked around to find Master Tarroc standing with the post in his hands.

"You're using this wrong," he said as he removed the rod that caused the radishes to drop on the floor. As I stood in silence, he grabbed the post and broke it in half before grabbing hold of one of the radishes. He grabbed the stem and pulled out an opened green vial, using it to fuse the top of the stem to the end of the post. Afterward he did that to the other end, and then finally to the other broken half of the post. He admired his invention before he looked over at me and tossed the two halves into the air towards me. They dropped at my feet as I examined the creations and wondered what I was supposed to do with them.

"What are these things?" I asked as I picked up the two things off the ground.

"They are called radishes," laughed TC as he briefly looked up from the grass stalks. Master Tarroc and I both looked back in disgust as TC quickly went back to focusing on his work.

"They are your radish chucks," replied Master Tarroc.

"Radish chucks?" I asked as my eyes examined them.

"Yes, now attack the individual scales as they poke out," replied Master Tarroc as he stepped back from the pinecone.

He stood in silence as I turned back towards the pinecone with a radish chuck in each hand. My mind suddenly began to release images of the foxes, which sent me into a rage as my hands grabbed tightly onto the radish chucks. I screamed loudly, which startled the moths out of the field as I launched an attack against the pinecone. Now, this part gets a bit hazy since I do not remember what happened other than I blacked out with the vision of Señor Saucy's face in my head. All I know is that there were a few minutes where I do not remember where I was and then I came to, only to see that I had a dead aim on a half-broken pinecone. I then blacked out again and came to on the side of the pinecone with bits of fur missing scratches on my arms. As the world stood in silence, I turned around to find myself in front of the empty shell of what was once a seed-filled pinecone. I turned to see TC, whose bug eyes were about to explode, and Master Tarroc next to him with his ears perked all the way up. Just as I was about to say something, the shell crumbled to the ground on top of the scales beneath it.

"Okay, what happened?" I asked.

"Not sure, but you just blew the nature off that pinecone," said TC as his eyes began to return to normal size.

"For a little rabbit, you have a lot of uncontrolled rage which, left to its own power, will injure both friend and foe," replied Master Tarroc as I stared downward upon my pulsing hands. I suddenly felt a tear roll down my furry cheek as I dropped the radish chucks onto the floor.

"What did I do?" I asked as I grabbed my ears in order to cover my face.

"I don't know, but whatever it was, it was the celery, son!" said TC as he raised a grass stalk high into the air.

"No need to cheer TC, he needs to control it before he can go and do what his mind wants," replied Master Tarroc as he walked over to me and placed his furry hand upon my back. He guided me to the shade. I reopened my waterlogged eyes and sat down as I laid my head against the wall of the trunk.

"I can't believe I did that," I said as I looked at the remnants of the pinecone being lifted into the air by the breeze.

"You definitely surprised us," replied Master Tarroc as he sat down next to me.

"So how do I control the anger?" I asked.

Master Tarroc paused for a moment, staring into the sky as he molded his goatee.

"There is no simple answer for such a complex question," he replied as he shut his eyes toward the sky.

His answer, of course, simply confused me even more than I was before. As he sat there in peace, TC finished the last pile and wiped the sweat from his green face. I watched as he grabbed hold of the snail shell he had on his back and lifted it to his face. He carefully chugged something down before dropping the shell on the ground to shatter into pieces. TC then began to walk over to the trunk's opening as I sat still as I let the wind swirl into my fur.

"Hey TC, can I ask you something?" I asked as he stopped just in front of the opening.

"You just did, but sure. What is it?" he replied with a bit of a smirk.

"Whatever happened to Briann and Trippe?" I asked. Instantly the smirk disappeared from his face.

"I have no idea, they disappeared after the foxes attacked the town," he replied as he dropped his head.

"I hope they are okay," I said as he began to walk inside of the trunk.

"Me too," he replied just before he disappeared into the trunk, leaving Master Tarroc and myself outside. I placed my head back upon the trunk as I watched the grass wave in the slight breeze. Just before I got up from the weedy soil, Master Tarroc exhaled and turned his head towards me.

"Where do you think you're going?" he asked with a bit of a grin.

"A place to get my rabbit thoughts back in order," I replied.

"Your training isn't done. You need to master yourself," he said as he pointed outward towards the open grass. I turned my head to see what exactly he was pointing at when I spotted the radish chucks, which were laid out on the ground next to the pinecone's remains.

"What do you want me to do with them?" I asked as I hopped over to the radish chucks. I bent down and was about to pick them up when suddenly a wail struck my ears. As my arms extended, I looked up to find Master Tarroc in midair with his stick pointed downward. I quickly grabbed the radish chucks and moved out of the way, just before his stick struck the ground. My heart was pounding as Master Tarroc removed his hood, his rabbit robe waving in the wind. He then charged at me with both hands upon the wooden stick above his head. I was barely able to get my radishes up before he violently swung the stick at me. The impact moved me back a bit as my radish chucks blocked his stick in the air. He snickered as he began to throw different stick strikes at me and I struggled to keep my defense up. After having successfully blocked some of his strikes, he suddenly kicked up some dust into my face and then laid me out with a strike to my back. The pain sent shockwaves through my back as he stood with a smirk.

"You cheated!" I yelled as I struggled to wipe the dust from my face and fight off the pain.

"You think the foxes will fight fair? They will do anything to hinder you," he replied. Of course, he was right, but that did not stop the anger from boiling upward as I rose to my feet.

"Now it's time for round two," I said as I turned around with a tight grip around my weapons.

Master Tarroc dropped back a couple of steps and readied the stick for another attack. My eyes reddened as this time I charged at him, one radish chuck above my head as the other dragged along the ground. Then, just before I attacked, I sprung into the air and jumped over Master Tarroc's head. He could just watch as I hung in the air, landing behind the wall of tall grass. I lowered my ears so he could not spot me, silently hopping around to the side of the hill. I stopped and popped my eyes over the edge as I watched Master Tarroc look all around.

"Come out, come out, wherever you are," he yelled aloud as he continued to look all around for me.

I grabbed my radish chucks tightly as I hopped behind a wall of the tall grass that stands around the trunk. I inhaled deeply as I exploded from in between the stalks of grass that had shielded me. To my surprise, however, the space was empty. My eyes bounced all over as I looked for Master Tarroc, hoping for a sneak attack. Before I could turn my head, suddenly a pain struck between my ears and then on my back, which sent me to the ground. As I shook the pain away, my eyes reopened to find Master Tarroc standing in front of me with his stick in hand.

"Nice try, but your lucky feet gave you away," he chuckled as he extended his hand out to me. I grabbed hold as he lifted me back to my feet.

"Once again beaten by the master," said TC as he walked back out into the open field.

"Yeah, well, I don't see you trying," I replied as I shook my head in disappointment.

"That is because my claws aren't sharp enough," replied TC as he lifted up his claws.

Before I replied, I suddenly spun around with my radish chucks, trying to catch him off guard. Just before I could hit him, he quickly jumped over my strike and then poked me in the chest.

"Nice try, young rabbit," said Master Tarroc as he hopped slowly towards the trunk where TC stood. I once again shook my head as I rubbed the part of my chest where he had poked me.

"You are just an immature rabbit who is simply a hare shorter than the rest," said TC as he flexed his buggy muscles.

As the anger inside built up, I watched Master Tarroc walk back, and my eyes wandered down to the pinecone's scales. Without a thought, I quickly picked up a scale, and with all my anger, launched it towards them. Just as he arrived at the trunk, the scale struck the wall, sending cracks in every direction. The force froze Master Tarroc in the opening as TC stared angrily at the scale lodged in the wall. TC then hustled over to it and then lifted his claw around the scale. He pulled it out and then threw it into the wall of grass beyond the hill.

"TC calm down. He is filled with anger far beyond any level we have ever seen," said Master Tarroc as he reached out to try to hold him back.

"No, this fool has to learn to respect his elders," TC replied as he lowered Master Tarroc's arm so he could step forward.

As Master Tarroc turned around, I angrily watched TC make his way over to the bent grass in front of me. His claws rattled and his eyes squinted as he glared at me. He stood in silence, and my hands gripped tighter onto the radish chucks as I waited for either of us to make a first move. He then charged at me with his claws open. Before he was able to attack, I hopped mightily back behind the grass where he had just thrown the scale into. As I stood with my back against the grass, I debated what my next big move would be against one of my brother's friends.

Before I could think anymore, one of his claws poked through the grass on each side of me. I quickly backed away, nearly tripping over the scale that had landed just before the edge of the hill. A smirk grew upon my face as I knelt down and opened my mouth, placing the scale on top of my tongue. I quickly shut my mouth just as TC poked his head through in between his claws. I quickly ran, hopping in and out of the grass. As I arrived at the clearing, I turned back to find TC had begun to tear through the grass using his claws as he approached me.

As the sun glistened off the sweat, he quickly cleaned his claws of all the remnants of grass. He smirked as he began to swing his claws at me. I blocked them with the radish chucks as I tried to look for an opening. His attacks nearly knocked me over the edge of the hill until I was able to trap his claws and push him out of my space. As I tried not to choke on the scale, I watched as TC dove at me in an attempt to knock me off the cliff. However, luckily, I managed to dodge him and hopped over to the other side of the trunk.

"How do you expect to beat the foxes if you can't even attack me?" TC yelled as he rushed through the breeze towards me. My eyes focused as he charged at me once again, but this time I just turned around in front of Master Tarroc. I shut my eyes as my ears shook at the sound of the ground, which vibrated as TC ran towards me. When the timing was right, I suddenly flicked my head up as I spit out the scale into the air as I drifted behind me. I kicked my feet outward, which influenced the scale and sent it flying flat into TC. Just as I turned around, I watched as the scale struck him in the face, which stopped him in his tracks. As he lay out on the ground, I turned around with my radish chucks out in front of my body. I made my approach as he groaned in agony on the ground, his claws clutching where the scale had hit him.

"That was definitely impressive and resourceful," said Master Tarroc as he appeared on my side. I took a step back as I watched TC lower his claws as he struggled to open his eyes.

"What in the open field did he do?" asked TC as he continued to groan in pain.

"The scale was mad at you," I chuckled as I watched TC slowly make his way back to his feet.

"Indeed it was, plus Pakul lured you into lowering your defenses," said

Master Tarroc as he tried hard not to laugh.

"Yeah, well, that was just luck," said TC as he tried to open his eyes a bit more.

"Yeah, well, that's why rabbits have two lucky feet," replied Master Tarroc as I looked down at my feet. I watched as he walked closer to TC and provided a crutch to help him stand.

"So am I ready to fight the Predators?" I asked as they began to walk closer to the trunk.

"Not yet, but you will be sooner than you think," replied Master Tarroc as TC raised his claw back to his head.

My head instantly dropped as I turned back around towards the line of cut grass. I could not help to wonder what the foxes were doing back in the Foxholes or why he did not think I was ready yet. My eyes wandered upward at the dusky sky as the sun began to sink toward the ground. I shut my eyes and sat amongst the breeze as the silence of the nature began to surround my furry body. However, before long, my peace was interrupted by a familiar poke into the side of my fur. My eyes reopened to find that darkness had settled onto the hillside, and a glow was coming from behind me. As I turned around, I found Master Tarroc standing just outside of the trunk, holding up a candle made from an old snail shell.

"Wow, darkness came fast," I said as I began to get up from the grassy ground.

"Yes, well, come inside. I wouldn't want you to be attacked by those mutated earthworms," replied Master Tarroc with a grin. My eyes widened as I quickly rose to my feet as I hopped over to him.

"Are you serious about those earthworms?" I asked as I hopped closer to the opening.

"Nope, just wanted you to hurry cause some of us want to call it a night," he replied with a chuckle.

"That wasn't funny," I replied as I hopped over to the bed that TC had made for me the night before. Just as I had made myself comfortable on my bed, Master Tarroc walked over to his chair and pulled out a drawer that sat next to it.

I watched as he placed down the shell candle and then picked up a box from out of the drawer. He placed it next to the candle and used his ear to remove the lid so he could see inside. His eyes gleamed by the candlelight at the sight of whatever he had seen in the box when suddenly he glanced over to me. I quickly shut my eyes to pretend I was sleeping. After a couple of seconds, I opened an eye a bit to find him sitting in his chair sleeping, with the box nowhere to be seen. The candle must have just gone out since the last bit of smoke was still floating away from the wick. I moved my eyes to the other side of the room when I spotted TC, who had stealthily made his way over to where Master Tarroc was sleeping.

"What do you think you are doing?" I whispered, making him freeze. He then hurried over to me and stopped directly next to the bed, which just allowed me to see the outline of his head.

"I want to see what he holds in that box, so stay quiet," he replied as he slowly made his way back over.

I watched as he arrived at the drawer and bent down to search for the box. However, after he searched for a bit, he raised an empty claw and returned to his side of the room. I wondered where the box had gone if it was not in there, or if maybe TC just was not looking hard enough. I shrugged it off as my eyes closed once again, this time sending me into a different world.

Suddenly, images filled the once-pitch-black sight that I had seen just moments after my eyes shut. I do not remember all the details, but I do remember that I was back in my Carrotminium with my family. Everything was normal, until the roof was removed, revealing Señor Saucy, who drooled when he saw me. Then, just before he reached in and ate me, my eyes suddenly exploded open as I woke up facing the side of the trunk.

Chapter 6

The next two days flew by quickly with my day packed with training as I tried to get the upper hand on Master Tarroc. On the third morning, my eyes opened to find myself in the same position as the previous two. As I lay on my bed, I watched as two shadows began to grow upon the wall I faced.

"Why good morning, Master Tarroc and TC," I said as I began to stretch.

"Morning, young rabbit, are you ready for your final lesson?" asked Master Tarroc as my eyes widened in surprise. I quickly spun around in order to face them as they stood next to my bed with a concentrated look in their eyes.

"Indeed, sir, I am ready and willing," I replied.

Master Tarroc turned to TC who turned towards him and then nodded his head as he looked back at me. As I tried to figure out what was going on, suddenly TC bent down and flipped over the bed, which trapped me between it and the wall.

"Okay and you did that why?" I asked as I tried to get from behind the bed. However, neither responded; instead all I heard was their feet as they scurried about on the wooden floor. As I headed towards one side, the back spines of a porcupine stopped me in my tracks. I turned around to the other opening, seeing a rodent who appeared to be holding a leaf that was reinforced with hardened mud.

"Now Pakul, this will require all the skills I have taught you, plus the control of your greatest emotion," said Master Tarroc from the behind the bed.

"Oh, and what would that be?" I asked as I continued to examine the rodent that stood in front of me.

"Fear," said TC as suddenly I looked up and watched as a carrot landed in between the rodent and me. Instantly, my mind filled with pain and the memories of my brother's demise that sent my head into a whirl. As the pain rose the flashbacks hastened, and I could feel the uncontrolled rage trying to explode through my skin.

"Now control the pain and make it a strength, otherwise you will be hindered in battle," said Master Tarroc as his voice rang through the buzzing in my ears.

I grimaced as tears began to fall from my eyes and I tried with all my might to get a handle upon the fear. I dropped to the floor as the memories worsened as the carrot laid there. I shut my eyes and everything went silent as the pain had sent me into a numbed state of mind. The blackness filled my sight as I tried unsuccessfully to move any of my limbs or even simply open my eyes.

"You can do it, brother," said a voice that was neither TC nor Master Tarroc. My eyes opened to find Lio standing in front of me as the rest of the world remained dark. He smirked as he turned towards me.

"Lio? Is that you?" I said as suddenly the pain began to fade out of my mind.

"Yep, I am the spirit of your lucky foot," said the spirit.

"I'm so sorry I just can't get past this fear of carrots," I replied as I hopped closer to my brother's spirit.

"You have no reason to fear them simply because of the Aquarrot. You must use it as motivation," said the spirit as it suddenly pulled out a carrot out from the air. My eyes widened as I prepared for the fear that was bound to occur however, nothing happened. I then watched, as the smirk grew larger and he then threw the carrot, which struck my chest and then landed upon the floor.

"What did you do that for?" I asked.

"Did the flashbacks hit you when you saw it?" he asked me. After a moment of thinking about it, I looked down at the carrot as it vanished back into thin air.

"No, they did not, but I don't understand," I replied.

"That is because your mind has come to realize a way to re-use your feelings towards the carrot in a better way," said the spirit as it began to fade away.

Suddenly, my eyes reopened to find myself back where I was, face to face with the rodent and the carrot at my feet. As my eyes caught a glimpse of the carrot, the newly found power rushed through my body as my eyes locked on to the rodent.

"Now Lamajo, charge him," said Master Tarroc as the rodent began to charge in my direction.

As he charged at me with leaf held high, my eyes shifted all over as I tried to find a way out. Then, as if my brother had thrown a mud ball at me, I quickly remembered the radish chucks that lay just on the other side of the bed. Just before he could strike, I slid on my stomach and managed to use my ear to knock one of radish chucks towards me. I quickly grabbed hold with both hands as the rodent stopped quickly before he met a painful poking. Lamajo then turned around and charged again as I braced myself for whatever he had planned. Just before he could bash my fur in, I quickly dropped the radish chuck onto the floor and began to hop onto the wall. I wall-ran until he blew past me, then I dropped to the floor and grabbed hold of the radish chuck. I quickly pulled the radish chuck, which took Lamajo's leg out from under him, sending him to the floor. Angry and his shield upon the floor, Lamajo brushed himself off as he turned towards me.

"Now for phase 2," said Lamajo as he snapped his claws together.

"Ok Caniya, back those spines up," yelled Master Tarroc from beyond the bed.

"All right it's time for the moonpine," replied Caniya as I watched as the spiny back began to inch closer towards me. My eyes widened as I spotted Lio's spirit once again, this time sitting upon the under sticks of the bed.

"Stop being a hare and be my brother," chimed his spirit just before it vanished.

Lamajo looked up to where I had stared to see nothing, but my brother's words renewed my belief. I watched as Lamajo picked up his shield and once again held it up as he walked towards me. I quickly walked back, keeping an eye on the painful spikes coming towards me. Before he could begin his charge, I quickly rushed at him and grabbed hold of the mud-encased leaf in order to take it from the rodent. As we tussled back and forth, I managed to pull it away from him even if my momentum nearly sent me into Caniya. I then looked down at the leaf and then at Lamajo who stood in disbelief in front of me.

"So you have it now, so what," chuckled Lamajo as he raised his claws into the air. He was right I had no idea; it was just something I did without even thinking. Then it suddenly it hit me, and I charged at the bed. I crashed through the middle of the bed, using the shield to protect me from the splinters. My body slid in front of Master Tarroc and TC, as I lay surrounded by the bed in pieces on the floor.

"My project!" yelled TC as he gathered the cardboard and twigs on the floor. I then quickly got up to turn around as I saw Lamajo and Caniya in shock at my actions.

"Well, we did tell him to be resourceful," shrugged Master Tarroc as he walked out of the opening of the trunk.

"Yeah well, we still get paid right?" asked Lamajo as Caniya looked on from his side.

Master Tarroc stopped as he turned around to look at TC who instantly stopped picking up the fragments. TC then grabbed a stone bowl filled with berries and brought it over to the two as they stood against the wall.

"Yes! I have thinking about this all morning," said Caniya as she took a sniff of the fresh berries inside the bowl.

"Now take your share and be on your own way," replied Master Tarroc as the two replied by nodding their heads as they looked down at the food.

They quickly inhaled the berries and ran past Master Tarroc just as he was about to step into the sunlight. Within a second, the two creatures were out of sight and TC went back to his job of picking up the pieces. I watched as Master Tarroc continued out of sight, which left me inside of the trunk along with TC, who kept his head down.

"Sorry for the mess, TC," I replied as I hopped out of the way.

"Just go outside and leave me be," replied TC. He did not even look up from the broken pieces on the ground.

As I quietly hopped my way outside, TC mumbled to himself as he continued the cleaning. Once I got outside, I looked around until finally I spotted Master Tarroc, back in his usual spot in the mossy shade. I hopped over to him as he grabbed a hold of a berry and raised it to his mouth. Just before I could sit down, he extended his arms out and pointed out to the grass.

"Now the second part of your final lesson will be for you to locate a berry similar to this one," said Master Tarroc as he raised the berry he held. He tossed the berry at me and for the first time I actually caught it, which in my brief life has not happened often. The berry was red with purple stripes up and down the sides with a blue top.

"I'll be right back," I replied as I hopped over the line of grass that TC cut up. As I arrived to the edge of the cliff, my eyes widened as beneath my furry feet stood lines of berries of all colors and sizes. With the berry in hand, I jumped downward into the field as I landed just outside the berry vines. My mouth watered at the sight of the plump and juicy berries, which lined up as we used to do when my mom cooked her special meal. I slowly walked along the lines as I looked for the correct match, but I was unable to find anything close to what Master Tarroc was looking for. There were berries of all colors but nothing close to what I was looking for and honestly, the thoughts seeped in if I would be able to find it. As I stood in front of the lines, suddenly the sound of chewing caused me to turn around towards the cliff. To my surprise, I found myself face to face with Lamajo and Camiya as they were eating the berries that Master Tarroc had given them. Then my eyes widened when I spotted the very berry I required in the hands of Lamajo who had begun to lick his lips at its sight.

"What, do you want this?" asked Lamajo as he took a firm grip on the berry in his hand.

"Yes I do, for Master Tarroc. So give it to me," I replied as I reached out my hand.

"If you want it then you have to get past my friend here," said Lamajo as he pointed over to Camiya who lifted her snout from bits of berry on the ground.

"Come on ears, or are you a chicken rabbit?" said Camiya as she slid down the cliff down to my level. I quickly charged at her as she suddenly turned around with her spikes faced at me. Before I met a pointy demise, I quickly dragged my feet in order to stop myself. Lamajo looked on with a smirk as I tried to figure out a way to get past his friend.

"Don't you want this berry?" yelled Lamajo as he moved the berry closer to his mouth.

My eyes quickly shot downward just in time to see Camiya as she attempted to ram into me. Just before she hit me, I hopped mightily out of the way as I watched as she slid to a stop. As the frustration began to set in, my eyes bounced all over as I could feel my desperation level as it grew.

"Use your surroundings, brother," said a voice that was instantly taken away by the wind.

I looked all around and found myself next to the very mud that had claimed me after I fell off the path. With a smirk, I hopped over to the mud and found a lone rose amongst the brown earth. Its beauty gleamed as I quickly hopped over and admired its natural defenses. The very thing that protected Camiya from me, I could use against her. After I had located the end of the thorns, I lowered my head and in one chomp released the rose from its roots. As the flower hung from my mouth, I quickly turned back to watch Camiya approach. Her eyes widened as she spotted me just as she began to charge in my direction. Then my plan had grown legs and had been set in motion, all I needed was for her to turn her back to me. Just as I had expected, she turned her back to me, which allowed me to drop the rose thorns upward onto the ground. I quickly jumped out of her path as I watched my plan come to fruition as Lamajo watched on.

"Watch out!" Lamajo yelled from the hillside.

However, he was too late, and I watched as Camiya's soft feet met the sharp thorns of my rosy trap. The instant that her feet stepped down all of her motion stopped as her attention turned to her foot. As she hopped around trying to shake off the pain, I made my move. I charged headfirst towards her to land a powerful tackle, which sent her backwards into the side of the cliff. The side vibrated upwards as it rattled Lamajo's body where he stood. Camiya looked at me as she tried to step forward but to my surprise, she was unable too.

"I'm stuck," said Camiya as she tried to wiggle her way loose from the wall.

"Yes, you are. Now Lamajo, it's your turn," I replied as I looked toward Lamajo.

His anger quickly boiled over as he watched Camiya using all of her might to pull herself free. With berry in hand, he jumped down next to Camiya and then charged at me as Camiya looked on. His rodent arms spread as he approached me but before he could hit me, I dodged it. Nothing spectacular, just a simple side-step where I just happened to keep a foot out which I used to trip him. Unable to stop, he tripped over my foot and went sliding headfirst into the very mud that once held the rose. As I held back a smile, I hopped onto his back sending him further into the mud. I then spotted the berry just out of his muddy paw's reach.

"Well this is going to be a dirty tale," I said as I hopped off Lamajo in order to safely land back on the grass.

As Lamajo groaned, I quickly picked up the berry. Having completed my mission, I walked with confidence back towards the cliff when I realized Camiya had vanished. I walked up to find that all that remained were several of her quills inside of little holes in the rocky side. I turned back to the mud to see that Lamajo had also disappeared. Without even a care about where they had gone, I began my ascent back up to Master Tarroc.

As I made my way back up, my mind was abuzz as it wondered what was in store for me back at the trunk. After I arrived at the top, I looked on just past the cut grass, as the outside of the trunk lay blank of any sign of Master Tarroc or TC. I began to look all around as I walked closer to it, trying to find a sign of them waiting for me. There was nothing though, just the usual wooden trunk and the dark entrance which led inside of it. As I held the berry close to my fur, I approached the entrance and slowly made my way inside the trunk. Then in relief, I found Master Tarroc as he sat in his chair while TC had begun to fix the bed I shattered.

"Do you have what I asked?" asked Master Tarroc as TC looked back at me. I revealed the berry in silence even though the berry still had specks of mud on its outer skin.

"Congratulations, you found a berry in a berry field," said TC as he returned his attention onto the bed.

"Just ignore him Pakul, and bring me that berry," he replied as I began to step closer to him. Just as I had gotten to him and was about to place the berry into his hand something cleared its throat. My eyes widened as I found a teary Camiya, and a muddy Lamajo standing in the trunk's opening.

"Okay, before they say anything, I didn't do it," I said.

"Oh, well then I can't say I'm impressed at the fact you defeated both by yourself," replied Master Tarroc.

"Not to interrupt, but yeah this was your trainee being resourceful," said Lamajo as Camiya continued to wipe the tears from her eyes.

"Impressive, even for someone who couldn't even escape from behind a leaf bed," said TC as he turned around to face us.

"Hey, I consider going through it escaping," I replied.

"Now don't you two start up again over that bed," said Master Tarroc as he poked the bed with his stick.

"Whatever, we just came to show you the trauma you have dealt to my friend here," Lamajo said as he extended a muddy hand to Camiya's back. He then broke a quill off just as some mud dripped off his arm onto the rim of the opening. More tears rolled down Camiya's snout as Lamajo showed us the broken quill, which was weakened by my attack.

"You realize that they will grow back, right?" said TC.

"Yes well, you shall never have Camiya and Lamajo to pick on," said Lamajo as he patted Camiya's back which caused another quill to break off. Camiya exploded in tears as she ran swiftly out of the trunk, which left Lamajo all alone.

"Now look at what you did," said TC as held back a smirk.

"I didn't mean to do that!" yelled Lamajo as he ran after Camiya into the open field. As they disappeared into the afternoon sun, Master Tarroc turned to me with a bit of smirk on his face.

"I just have one question for you," said Master Tarroc

"Ask away," I replied as he rose out of the chair and turned towards me.

"How did you do that to Camiya?" asked Master Tarroc as he scratched the hairs on his chin.

"Just simply with a rose," I replied as confusion crossed his face.

"You just might be ready to venture to the Foxholes," said Master Tarroc which caused TC to stand up.

"Master, are you sure?" asked TC.

Master Tarroc stood silently as he looked at me and then quickly turned back to TC as he nodded his head. TC nodded back and went back to work on the bed as I began to think about what exactly I had just gotten myself into. I mean really, I might have been good, but did he honestly believe I could handle Señor Saucy at that time?

"Are you sure there is nothing else I can learn?" I asked as my nerves continued to grow.

"Well, there is one thing you haven't done," replied Master Tarroc as he grabbed my radish chucks from the floor. He tossed them at me and began to stare at me as I held them in my hand.

"Was that it?" asked TC with a chuckle.

"Will you stop being a wisebug for a moment," replied Master Tarroc. TC nodded his head as a smirk grew on my face, which caught the attention of

Master Tarroc.

"You shall battle me to one fall," he continued as he pointed out to the afternoon sun that beamed even brighter.

I took a deep breath and made my way outside as I wondered how in the world I could beat him. As I waited, he appeared in the opening with his stick in hand and his eyes focused upon me. My breath quickened as I watched him step closer as he raised his stick into the blue sky above him.

"When are we starting?" I asked as I took a couple paces backward.

He smirked and then charged at me with the stick floating in mid-air as it shredded through the wind. I quickly gulped and watched as the stick barely missed my nose as it landed in the dirt near my feet.

"Now," he said as he re-raised the stick once again and prepared for another strike.

However, this time I had it because I was able to block it with a radish chuck as I sent his stick into the grass. Our eyes followed the stick into the grass when suddenly I was sent backward as he kicked me in the stomach and he ran to it. I shrugged it off as I watched him pick it up just as he slid near the edge. He charged at me once again as he fired off strike after strike and I began to strike back. Our strikes blocked each other's until he changed it up when he swept my feet out from under me.

As I rose back to my feet, he hopped back, allowing me room to get myself back upright. Just as I had gotten my wits, he charged at me again but this time I was ready. I countered with a sidestep as I hit him with a shoulder bash, which sent him into his shady spot. He nodded his head just before he hopped mightily into the blinding sunlight above me. Before I was even able to look for him, he landed a shot to my back that caused me to stumble into the trunk's side. I quickly dodged his weapon as I managed to turn around in time to cause it to break some leaves loose. The leaves began to fall as I tried to regain my breath while Master Tarroc stood up against the trunk's side. As the final leaf struck the ground, Master Tarroc charged again. I kept on the defense even as every swipe sent me a step back towards of the cliff. Before I went any further, I ducked under his attack and then chopped his knee with one of my radish chuck. His knee came within inches of the ground as I quickly hopped away as I wondered what I could do.

"That was the best you can do?" asked a voice.

This time it did not sound like my brother, instead TC chirped from the entrance of the trunk. Rather than make eye contact with him, I kept my focus on Master Tarroc who rose back up. Before he turned towards me, I quickly jumped into the line of cut grass out of his view. As I watched through the blades of grass, Master Tarroc began to walk towards where I once stood.

"Very predictable, young rabbit, but I have seen this move before," he said as suddenly jabbed his stick in between the blades of grass. The stick went just above my head and in between my ears as I tried to remain quiet. I quickly spotted a rock at my feet, which I knocked down the line of grass as I used my radish chuck to hit it. It flew down the line, which ruffled the grass when he pulled back his stick.

"Okay, now what?" I asked myself as I tried to see what I could do.

"Oh come on I refuse to believe you don't have any creativity in you," said a voice.

I looked to my right and found my brother's spirit as he peeked through the blades of grass. He shut the grass and turned towards me with a smirk as he suddenly disappeared again. Suddenly, my eyes widened when I saw a fallen pinecone that had lost some of its scales on one side. I hopped over to it and stepped into the empty space in order to give myself some cover. Then it came to me, I quickly placed the scales back one by one until they loosely covered the space. As I tried to hold them still, I used my feet to hold the bottom two still and my mouth to hold the top one in place. This kept the wall in place as I watched Master Tarroc walk over to where he had nearly hit me. He bent down and picked up some of my fur that had shed while I had hid there.

"You have to be here somewhere," he said as I tried to remain perfectly still. My nerves reached their peak as I watched him walk towards the unstable wall as he looked all around the pinecone for a sign of me.

"Remember the bed," said a voice inside of my head.

Then just as he turned his back towards the pinecone, I let go of the three scales that sent the entire side downward onto Master Tarroc. Just as he turned around, he began to be struck by the scales and then finally my fluffy rabbit body splashed on top of him. He crumbled to the ground as I managed to hop away from the falling scales. After the last one had fallen, TC ran out of nowhere to kneel at Master Tarroc's side as he struggled to get up.

"You're an animal," TC said to me as he reached out a claw to help Master Tarroc get back to his feet. As he struggled to stand, TC allowed himself to be used as a brace as he tried to shake off the dizziness. After his eyes lost the glazed look, he quickly honed in on me as I stood to his side.

"Congratulations Pakul, you have bested me," he whispered as he hobbled over to the trunk.

I smirked as they made their way over to the trunk's safety while I turned and looked over the cliff. "I don't know how Lio, but I love having you to guide me," I said into the empty space as it echoed through the plains below.

PAKUL

As the wind carried my voice away, I turned around with radish chucks in hand and hopped toward the trunk.

Chapter 7

Now this part furthered my mission against the Predators, and their slimy leader Señor Saucy. As we prepared to call it a night inside the trunk, Master Tarroc sat down upon his chair and opened up the drawer. He swiftly pulled out the box that he had pulled out that other night. I watched as he held the box firmly as his eyes began to look at me.

"I have something to show you," he said as he rose out of the chair and began to walk over to me. As he held the box firmly against his chest fur, he made his way to my side as he sat upon the bed. The bed gave a bit as he sat down but it quickly adjusted as Master Tarroc looked down upon the box.

"What is it?" I asked as he placed the box upon my lap.

"Open it and find out," he replied as he got up from the bed.

He turned around, however I barely noticed as my hands crept over to the top of the box. I lifted the top and moved it to the side as my eyes quickly zoned in on the contents of the box. Inside the box was a dusty amulet that had bit of an orange stain to it as well as the bottom of the box. I slowly lifted the amulet out from the box and brought it closer to my eyes so I could examine it. This amulet appeared awfully familiar from the length to the rabbit insignia located at the heart of the amulet.

"This looks familiar," I said as I continued to look at the amulet with intent.

"That is because it was Lio's," said TC from out of the trunk's shadows. My eyes widened as I stared at the amulet as my eyes filled with tears.

"Indeed it was, however we found it near the roads just outside of Tortabbi," said Master Tarroc as he placed his furry hand upon my shoulder.

"I bet the foxes dropped it," added TC as he prepared his area for sleep. A tear or two dropped from my eyes onto the amulet which took away some of the dust that had settled down on it.

"It doesn't matter now, it's yours so you can always remember him," said Master Tarroc as he grabbed the amulet out of my hands. I watched as he lifted it up and then proceeded to place it around my neck as he backed away.

"How does it look?" I asked as I began to adjust it a bit.

"You look a rabbit destined for greatness," replied Master Tarroc as he walked back over to his chair.

As I cleared the final tear from my eye, I watched as he sat back into his chair while TC disappeared from the light in the room. I quickly lay back on the bed as my hands grasped a gentle hold upon the amulet and my eyes shut. It was not long until I was suddenly jarred awake by TC's massive claws as smoke and embers began to fill inside.

"Get out of here now! Those crazy foxes are trying to cook us alive!" yelled TC as he quickly jumped off my bed. The walls had grown an orange glow as the main opening had been blocked by flames. I quickly turned towards TC who had followed Master Tarroc towards the ingrown bark, which led up to the hole in the roof.

"Pakul, come and exit out of the hole in the top!" said Master Tarroc as he pointed upward.

I quickly hopped around the swirling bark as TC pulled the vine, which allowed the top to open. Just as I had managed my way through the hole, I quickly turned back to grab hold of whoever was next. However, before either of them could climb up a large red fox walked through the flames that had no effect upon him. My eyes froze as suddenly two smaller foxes jumped through flames, joining the larger one inside.

"Where is he?" asked the large fox as the two smaller ones began to chuckle.

"I don't know who you are talking about, Char," replied TC. Before I could see anything further, TC let go of the vine that closed the top and held me out of any view. I quickly dropped my ear to the lid to see if I could overhear anything from inside the room.

"I know he is here, mantis. Don't lie to the Predators," said Char.

"I have no reason to lie," replied TC as suddenly I begin to hear the cackle of the smaller foxes.

"What about you, the supposed rabbit master?" asked Char as I could hear Master Tarroc as he released a cry of pain.

"Your time is up, foxes. He shall come for you," replied Master Tarroc which kicked a mighty chuckle out of Char and the other two.

"You two grab these fools and throw them outside before us all burn," said Char as I quickly realized myself that the flames had grown all over the trunk.

Just as I had begun to panic, I hopped all around as I tried to find a way to escape without being captured. However, on every side were foxes whose eyes glowed red as the fires burned all around the trunk. Trapped with no way down, I looked down to find Char as he dragged Master Tarroc and TC by their necks towards two cages. One by one, he threw them inside as he laughed menacingly when suddenly the trunk below me began to crumble. My feet began to vibrate as I watched the floor beneath crash to the ground while the foxes ran off as their rabbit transportation dragged my friends away.

Just before I could find a way to safety, the floor dropped and sent me downwards back onto the room. I fell flat upon where my bed had stood just before my eyes shut and things went silent. When I came back to, I could barely move my body that lay prone and covered by the fragments of the bark from the trunk. The sun above provided some light into my situation as it leaked in from the cracks of the bark. I was somewhat surprised because I lacked pain, even as I noticed the bit of blood that dripped just below my ear. I looked around as I found myself unable to lift myself out of the ruins that had encased me. Before I could think about how I could get out of this predicament, something grabbed a hold of my leg. It gently pulled me out of the trap. Once all of my body was out, I struggled to my feet when I turned around to find a bird just a bit larger than myself.

"Are you food?" asked the bird as it tilted its head at me.

"No the name is Pakul, what is yours?" I replied as I wiped the blood away from my eye.

"Name is Montavious Doarrennur," said the bird as it kept its keen eyes on me.

"That's a weird name. Do you have a nickname, Montavious?" I asked as I reached to my sides to find my radish chucks nowhere to be found.

"My friends call me Monty," replied Monty as I hopped on top of the ruins in search for my weapons.

I searched through all the bits of bark until I almost gave up when I came across them laid out by where the opening of the trunk would have been. As I reached in and grabbed hold of them, I hurriedly moved them back to my sides as I scooted back to safety. Once off the ruins I found myself once again face to face with Monty who had rushed over to my location.

"Can I help you?" I asked innocently as the bird continued to stare upon my furry body.

"Just looking for some food," he said swiftly as he turned his head towards the bottom of the cliff. I then watched as Monty's eyes widened and his feet began to jump up and down in excitement at whatever he had spotted.

"What do you see?" I asked as I looked in the direction of where he was looking.

"Food," replied Monty as suddenly he ran off the side of the cliff downward onto the plains below. I scurried over to the edge where I found Monty just as he began to attack the plots of field berries. I had never seen someone go through food like that since my siblings and I gulped down my parent's carrot special. After about the fifth shrub, Monty stopped and let out a massive burp as he went back onto his path of eating destruction.

"Wow, he should have been named Vacuum," I said as I turned my attention and focus back to the foxes that had taken my friends.

The blood had dried itself upon my fur, as the path ahead appeared familiar. It came back to me that it was the path that had brought us to Tortabbi. I looked down upon my radish chucks and then looked back as I began to hop my way down the road towards my former hometown. My mind filled with questions as I began to set off with my radish chucks at my side. For example, how I planned to get into the foxhole without being stewed or exactly how I planned to beat the entire group by myself. As I got to the bend in the pathway, I stopped for a second and looked over to find that the berries had bested Monty, who was now plopped on the floor.

I shook my head and hopped along the road to my hometown as I passed through the open fields of grass on both sides. It had become even more peaceful than usual since the events of last night but even now my mind couldn't get over what I was going to do. As I reached a little bit farther away from Monty, my eyes spotted what I originally believed to be a fox head. I quickly gathered my radish chucks as I increased my hop towards its location. As I had gotten halfway there, the things vanished before I could get a good look, so I hurried more with a tighter grip. I then made my approach as I slowed down just in case this was something fishy so I jumped into the opening with radish chucks ablaze.

"Hey you, its Pakul right?" said Lamajo from inside of a cage similar to the one they placed Master Tarroc and TC in. As I lowered my weapons, I realized that right next to a still muddy Lamajo was Camiya who wept in the corner of the cage.

"Well, if it isn't the two runaways," I replied as I walked up to the front part of the cages.

"Kind of hard to run away when you're trapped in a cage," replied Lamajo.

"What's wrong with her?" I asked as I pointed over to Camiya.

"Nothing, and how about you stop your blubbering," yelled Lamajo as Camiya wiped the tears from her eyes.

"Will you just tell him that we are the ones who sent Char and his gang to the stump?" cried out Camiya as Lamajo slowly turned to me. My anger rocketed and I'm sure steam exploded out of my ears after I heard this.

"Why in the world would you do such a thing?" I asked as I began to shake the cage Lamajo was in. The cage bounced up and down as Lamajo barely managed to keep his rodent feet on the ground.

"We didn't know," replied Camiya as I stopped, allowing Lamajo to capture his breath.

"Yeah man, we didn't. They came to us as rabbits and then next minute we were in here," said Lamajo as he smacked the cage bars.

"What do you mean?" I asked as Lamajo turned around towards the back of the cage which revealed the scars on his back.

"Char burned us with those evil little fox friends of his," said Lamajo as he reached a hand back to feel the scars.

"Yep, and Lamajo took a lot until he finally cracked…we are sorry," replied Camiya as she reached a hand through the cage towards Lamajo. His head dropped in sadness as his hand extended as he grabbed hold of hers. My eyes watered as Lamajo's tears dropped down through the sticks in the floor.

"I'm sorry and I will get our revenge," I said as I quickly hopped off.

"Wait, you aren't going to free us?" asked Camiya. I turned around to see them both as they grasped onto the stick wall of the cage.

"Let me see what I can do," I replied as I hopped back over to examine the cages they were in. They were simply designed with just sticks and vines from around the trees around the field tying them together. As I walked up to the wall, Lamajo backed up to allow me some space to work. I picked up my radish chucks and began to wail upon the sticks which just led me to tire out. After I managed to chip bits away, I came up with a new idea, so I hopped upwards onto the top of the cage.

"What are you going to do?" asked Lamajo as he squatted along the floor.

"Not sure yet," I replied as he looked at the edges of the top part of the cage.

"You have buck teeth why don't you chew through the wood," said Lamajo.

"Here is some breaking news: I am a rabbit not a beaver," I replied as I went to focusing on the task.

"Ok I am going to use my radish chucks to remove the vines," I said as I took a tiny hop towards one of the corners. Just as I landed, I heard the sticks a bit as they sent some splinters downward which put a smile on my face.

"What happened?" asked Camiya as she looked on from her cage.

"Ok Lamajo, I want you to cover your face. I am going to try something," I replied as Lamajo began to cover his face. Then as Camiya looked on, I suddenly rose my hind feet upwards and then sent them with all my force downward. Of course, thinking about it now, I should have protected myself because the sticks broke which sent me through the cage. As my feet landed, the sticks shattered which sent not just their fragments but me as well downward onto the floor. I fell through the bottom part two joined this time by Lamajo who uncovered his face just as he landed on the bottom.

"Are you guys ok?" asked Camiya as she tried to get a peek at us through the sides of the cage.

"I'm ok," groaned Lamajo as he shook off the pieces of sticks and vines that covered parts of his fur.

"How about you Pakul?" asked Camiya as Lamajo made his way out of the rubble. I shook off the dizziness as I rose to my feet to find Camiya as she stared at me through her cage's bars.

"I'll be fine," I replied as I gingerly proceeded out of the rubble.

Lamajo and I quickly turned to his cage with a bit of a smirk at the sight of the broken frame that lay below it. We then turned our attention to Camiya who began to grow nervous as she stared at the roof of her cage.

"I am not doing that again," I said as I began to examine her cage for a different strategy.

"Why not? I mean, this time I can pull you to safety before you fall," said Lamajo as he walked over to the cage's ruins. I watched as he bent down and pulled out one of the vines that had once held his cage together.

"Let's do it," I said as Lamajo tossed me one of the ends to the vine.

Lamajo then walked over and tied it around me as I jumped up to the top of the cage. I then looked down to find that Camiya had already covered her face in preparation for my break in. As I took a deep breath, I lifted up my legs and sent them smashing through the roof of the cage. Just as I began to fall, I was suddenly stopped thanks to Lamajo on the outside holding me steady. I then looked down to find clear air as Camiya looked back up at me unharmed.

"Ok Lamajo, lower me and I'll tie it around Camiya so you can free her, then you can free me," I said as Lamajo got closer which allowed me to reach Camiya's level. With my feet firmly against the floor, I removed the vine and tied it around Camiya so she could be lifted out. I then watched as Lamajo struggled to lift her up as she slowly rose up and over the side of the cage. As her feet settled onto the ground, Lamajo helped remove the vines carefully avoiding her spines. Lamajo then looked down upon at the vine and then turned to me as I stood behind the walls of the cage.

"You can free yourself," said Lamajo as he threw the vine away to the shock of Camiya.

"What are you doing? He helped us!" asked Camiya.

"Yeah well that was his fault not ours," replied Lamajo as he began to walk away from me.

"You're just going to leave him here?" asked Camiya as she stood still.

"Yes, so either you come with me or join him in a useless fight," replied Lamajo as he stopped his stride. Camiya looked back at me and then turned towards Lamajo as she was clearly torn about what she should do.

"Go. He is right, this is my battle," I said.

Camiya nodded her head and then began to walk over to Lamajo who stood with a smirk.

"Well Pakul, thanks but now once again you are by yourself," replied

Lamajo as he and Camiya walked off quickly through the brush leaving me alone.

With them gone, my thoughts quickly turned to how in the world I would free myself from this cage. Then my eyes widened as I grabbed hold of the vine in order to tie to a stick on two sides of the cage. Once the vine was secured, I gently placed one of my feet on it as I crashed my other downward onto the stick bottom. Like I predicted, the sticks broke and dropped as I somehow managed to hold my balance on the vine. Once all the pieces had landed, I hopped off the vine and landed safely on the ground without a scratch.

"That was lucky," said a voice from out of nowhere. My eyes turned all around until I spotted my brother's spirit standing next to me.

"How are you everywhere I am?" I asked as I turned towards him.

"Simple, foolish one. Anywhere there is wind I can reach you or at least until you defeat the saucy one," replied Lio.

"So then I guess I'm never alone then," I replied.

"Afraid not, bro," he said just as he faded into the gust of wind that passed by.

Before I continue down the road, my eyes suddenly caught a glimpse of smoke in the sky located just west of where my hometown sat. I quickly looked down at my radish chucks which sat to my sides while the amulet still hung around my neck. My mind flew with wonder at what had caused the smoke or what exactly it could lead me too.

"It starts now," I said aloud as I continued down the road when I suddenly steered myself into the shrubs.

Of course you might ask why, well it's simple they would be expecting me to take the road up to the main gate. That, and there was something about that smoke that really screamed out at me to check it out. So as I continued on my way through the over grown grass, my eyes were blinded by a reflective surface. As I looked back to the area it shined a bit, which caused me to head over to it. The object continued to shine which allowed me to maneuver through the grass even as my eyes squinted from the reflected light. Once I arrived, I found myself looking at what appeared to be some sort of metallic sign. I looked down and found myself staring at an extremely inaccurate poster of myself.

In large print the poster read "TO ALL PREDATORS" and on the bottom was "WANTED". A smirk came upon my face at the thought that I was apparently important enough to be wanted. After the initial happiness, the feeling began to sour at the thought of the expected battles ahead in order to maintain my rabbit freedom. My head shook as I kicked some dirt upon the poster as I once again took off towards the smoke. As I aimed my sights ahead, the smoke began to plume upwards with less intensity as it once did. I watched as it got closer to me and then finally I was just beyond some brush that stood between me and the source. I heard no voices, so I poked my head through the holes in the brush where I found a very unwelcome sight. Just beyond laid Char and his gang of foxes around a recently burnt-out fire. As I continued to examine the camp, I glimpsed upon some friends of mine inside some cages. It was Master Tarroc and TC; they were lying down on the bottom of the cage with TC's claws tied together.

"You better hide," said a voice as I watched a ladybug fly from out of the brush.

I quickly realized why I needed to hide since making a round was a fox camp guard who had begun to approach my area. As I tried to figure out what to do, I quickly rushed backward into the overgrown grass and dropped to the dirt. I lay still as I held my ears while I watched the guard walk towards where I had just stood. It walked up to it and then stopped as it suddenly began to look around for what I took as a sign of me still being around. I exhaled as it shook its head and continued to walk out of my sight from the grass.

I slowly lifted myself up from the ground and began to step out from the grass. As I peeked down the path where the guard had walked, I managed my way towards the brush at the camp's edge. Once again, I poked my head through the grass and watched as the foxes began to wake up from their naps and stretched with a howl. Char and the two from the trunk were closest to the Master Tarroc, while the rest surround the camp with their leafy shelters. As I watched them awaken, I quickly wondered how I could free them without having myself captured in the process.

Chapter 8

As my brain wandered, I kept my sight upon the camp as the foxes began to gather near Char.

"So what shall we do with these?" asked one of the smaller foxes to Char.

Char looked back at TC who was still down and then turned towards him to shake the cage violently. TC kept smacking into the sides since his hands were tied while Master Tarroc tried to grab hold as his cage shook a bit as well. The foxes laughed as Char pulled back which allowed to TC to gather his balance inside the cage.

"I say we remove his claws permanently and then place him in a field for the birds," replied Char as the rest of the foxes cheered in approval.

"Please don't," said Master Tarroc which suddenly quieted the crowd. Char grew angry as he turned to Master Tarroc, whose elder state had left him in the center of the cage.

"How dare you talk out of place, you pathetic excuse for a creature," replied Char as his anger began to boil over. My rage began to bubble as I watched helplessly as Char turned his attention back to TC.

"So Captain, shall we prepare the prisoner for his sentence?" asked a fox when suddenly a dragonfly dropped into the camp.

The foxes and I watched as the dragonfly came in and landed upon the top of TC's cage with what appeared as a message in its mouth. It then quickly spit out the message into Char's hand as it quickly flew away out of the camp. Char then unrolled the message and then looked it over when he raised his head with a smirk.

"It appears that the talk of Rabbit Avenger was nothing more than a figment of an old rabbit's tale," said Char as he dropped the note to the ground.

The foxes erupted in a cheer as Char turned back to TC who stood nervously in the back of the cage. Char directed two foxes to the side of the cage as he looked on while they jumped on top of the cage. Helplessly I looked on as the two foxes threw back the top and jumped inside the cage. They grabbed hold of TC's buggy legs and boosted him over the cage side to where Char grabbed a hold of him. Char then lowered him down onto the shoulders of some of the foxes as TC struggled to try and get away.

"Don't show them weakness and save your energy, apprentice," said Master Tarroc. TC stopped moving as the foxes dropped him down at the feet of

Char who snarled at the sight.

"Some strength from a rabbit inside of a cage," replied Char.

I stood frozen as I watched Char as he walked over to the fire and pulled out a rock from the bottom of the smoke. He laughed as he struggled to raise the rock above his head as he walked over to TC. He stopped in front of his claws which were being held down and extended the rock fully into the air.

"Stop, don't do this Char! Remember the nice fox you used to be!" yelled Master Tarroc just as Char was about to drop the rock.

"Don't worry, you are next," replied Char as he once again raised the rock back over TC's claws.

"I have to do something before they hurt him," I whispered as I tightened my grip upon my weapons of choice.

Suddenly just as I had placed one foot down into the camp, something grabbed hold of me and sent me backwards out of the brush. Before I could yell anything, a hand quickly covered my mouth before I could get a word out.

"You and your friend will be safe," whispered the voice in my ear as I relaxed a bit. The creature removed his furry hand and let me loose which allowed me to turn around. My eyes widened when I came face to face with two rabbits whose scarred-riddled fur looked back at me.

"You are rabbits," I said low enough so I wouldn't have given myself away.

"Yes, we are. Now gather your weapons the fight is about to start," said the rabbit as the other ran up to the brush he was pointing to.

I then turned around and followed him to the brush as we both poked our heads through to see the camp. Our sight found Char as he just finished mocking TC and was now about to drop the rock onto the prone claws. Then it happened as I watched on, just as Char let go of the rock a spear of sharpened asparagus launched out from the other side of the camp. It struck Char's hand and then smacked into the ground just to the side of the empty cage.

My eyes widened as suddenly some animals rushed into the camp with their weapons drawn. Before I could even respond, the rabbits next to me rushed through the brush with their carrot daggers drawn. One by one the animals began the fight with the foxes which left Char stunned as he back away from TC. This band of animals swarmed the camp and began taking the foxes down one by one. As I watched from the ringside, I found myself shocked when I located a familiar face amongst the group. It was Camiya with a back full of quills except for two which she held as weapons in her hands.

It was a sight to watch her fight off numerous attackers and be victorious as she dealt the fatal blow with those barbed quills. The rest of the group was a bunch of unfamiliar faces that not only defeated them swiftly but pushed them out of the camp. I continued to watch as Char quickly rushed out his troops as he managed to send one of the group members into Master Tarroc's cage.

"You fools think you have won, but you are sadly mistaken," roared Char as he quickly followed his fox groupies out of the campsite.

As I figure that this was probably the right time, I jumped out from the bushes and began to hop up and down at the victorious group. Startled, they turned towards me with their weapons still drawn but now in my direction. I quickly raised my hands at the group when suddenly Camiya broke from the group and walked over to me. She dropped the quills onto the floor and got close to me with a bit of a smirk on her face.

"It is ok, this is Pakul. He rescued me from the cage," proclaimed Camiya as she turned back to the group.

The group roared as they lowered their weapons and some turned back to free Master Tarroc from his cage. As they broke the cage open, Master Tarroc stepped out with thanks of each animal while some removed the vines from TC's claws. As the two got encircled by the group, Camiya and the rabbit from earlier stepped in my direction. The rabbit dropped the cloth that covered his mouth which revealed a patch of brown fur similar to my brothers'.

"My name is Bucky Tailfur," said the rabbit as he wiped the sweat from above his eyes. Suddenly, something about that name sent my mind into a flashback and then it hit me.

"Are you the same Bucky from down the street?" I asked as Camiya turned towards Bucky.

"You wouldn't happen to be the Carrotear son that went missing a long time ago?" asked Bucky as he walked closer.

"That's me, well one of them," I replied.

"Wait, one of them?" asked Camiya as she took a step back.

"Yeah, the story was two went missing and never returned," replied Bucky.

"I'm the only one remaining," I said as Camiya listened on.

"That is true, however I don't remember them having a purple-furred son," replied Bucky as he circled around me.

"That is a long story which includes the loss of a loved one," I said back as my eyes followed him as he walked around me. Before he could respond, Master Tarroc stepped from out of the group followed by TC who continued to shake the feeling back into his claws.

"We must remove ourselves from this area, I fear they will return in greater number," said Master Tarroc as Bucky stopped and turned towards him.

"I will agree with you. Come, let's head down to our hideout just a mile or two down from here," replied Bucky as he hastily rushed out of the campsite with his group directly behind him. Just as they had all about left, Camiya began to walk out when she suddenly stopped and turned back towards me.

"Are you not coming?' asked Camiya as I looked back towards the direction of my former home.

"I need to defend the honor of my brother and find my family," I replied as I turned a bit into its direction.

"Yeah well, you would be a total fool to just go," said TC who appeared from the brush. I turned towards him as he stood at the edge of camp while Camiya walked past him.

"You of all should now that I need to avenge him," I replied as TC shook his head.

"That's true, but I also know it's not the right time," replied TC as Camiya disappeared into the brush. My head dropped as his words settled inside with the realization that he was right about this.

'So what should I do?" I asked as I raised my sight back up.

"Come back with us," replied Bucky as he poked his head out from the brush.

"We're coming," I said as I began to walk towards TC at the other side. TC smirked as I got closer and then turned around to walk out of the campsite. As we came out of the campsite, Bucky placed his hands on our shoulders and nodded as we walked all together through the overgrown grass.

"Just wondering, where we going?" asked TC as he turned to a hopping Bucky.

"To New Hareville," he replied as our eyes widened in shock.

As we walked together, the grass seemed to never end because just when you thought you were out it just got deeper. Then finally after having walked for what felt like forever, Bucky hopped ahead of us in order to reach a wall of weeds. He then stopped and turned around to us with a giant smirk which reached both of his rabbit cheeks.

"Welcome to New Hareville," said Bucky as he bent back the grass to reveal a snakeskin door which connected finely thin walls. As we walked closer, we watched as spiders streamed more webbing upon the wall as the snakeskin pulled away to allow us inside.

"What are they doing?" asked TC as he pointed to the spiders.

"They are making our town safer," replied Bucky as I began to examine the insides of the city. This town felt nothing like old Hareville did, especially since that most of the animals were not rabbits. I watched as the worker ants worked on building up the outskirts as we began to approach the building which had the most action. It appeared to have walls built from leaves and old animal bones while the roof appeared to be a flipped over bird's nest. We walked up to the doorway and stepped inside where the rest of the camp's group awaited our arrival. They cheered as we stepped inside either for the fact that we had arrived or for their victory, but I didn't care. A smile lit my face as we walked closer and Bucky quickly silenced the crowd.

"Chalk that up for victory!" yelled Bucky which the crowd responded with a massive roar. TC and I looked on in awe as Bucky walked up to the animals and thanked them for their assistance. One by one, they walked away which left us three alone in the main room. Bucky then proceeded to the second floor when suddenly two soldier ants appeared from the door next to the walkway.

"Sire, the prisoners request to see the purple rabbit," said one of the ants as they saluted him. Bucky stopped and turned around to see TC and me standing still in the main room next to where the ant stood.

"Well there he is, you can ask him yourself," replied Bucky as he turned back around and hopped out of my view. I turned around as the ant dropped the salute and then turned to me as it began to kneel.

"Oh radish rabbit, please excuse me I didn't see you there," the ant said as it continued to bow in front of me. As a confused look began to pop on my face, I turned to TC who had a smirk as he watched the ant.

"It is quite ok, and please call me Pakul," I replied as the ant looked up from the ground.

"He talked to me," whispered the ant to the other ant who kneeled by the side door.

"Did you become a hero and you didn't tell me?' asked TC as he crossed his arms.

"Yeah, it's because I wiped out an entire army of rabid ferrets which had escaped from a radioactive plant," I replied as I jokingly flexed my muscles.

"Not to interrupt but sir would you mind visiting a prisoner," asked the ant as the other one opened the spider webbed door.

"Sure why not," I replied as I shrugged my shoulders and began to hop towards the door as the ant led the way. As the ants and I walked down the ramp, a slight wind brushed our back which caused us to turn around. As we turned, we found TC in the doorway with the spider silk door collapsed at his feet.

"This wasn't me, it was a dung beetle I tried to catch him," replied TC as he looked down at his feet.

"Have someone fix that. We wouldn't any prisoners breaking free," whispered the ant to the other as it sped through TC's legs.

"Just admit it, you wanted to come," I said to TC.

"I would love to," replied TC as he quickly scurried over next to me and the ant. I shook my head as once again we continued our descent into the musty darkness which crippled this part of the building.

"Where are we?" I asked as I continued to look around at the soiled walls which led us to a line of doors.

"It's their flower garden," replied TC as he let out a brief chuckle which stopped once he saw he had not achieved a smirk from either of us.

"You're close; this is where we hold our rule breakers," said the ant as we passed the first door and walked up to the second one. As we arrived at the door, we stopped and turned towards it as the ant crawled up next to the doorknob.

"Wait, who is this prisoner?" asked TC as he tried to sneak a peek behind the door.

"It's prisoners, and would one of you mind opening the door now that I have unlocked it," replied the ant as TC and I looked at one another.

"Go ahead, hero," said TC as he took a step back from the knob.

As I stared at him as I tried to digest his sarcasm I stepped forward to the doorknob. I then took a deep breath and reached out the knob as it creaked when I began to open it. Once I had fully turned it, the mud door slid open slowly as TC and I tried to get a sight. Just as the door had fully opened, the ant jumped off and walked inside as we stood in the doorway filled with curiosity.

"Alrighty jokester and accomplice, we have brought you the radish rabbit," yelled the ant into the darkened part of the room.

TC and I both took a step forward into the room as my fur began to shake as my nerves hit. Then out of the darkness a loud creaking sound filled my ears which caused me to brace. Just before we could do anything else, two animals appeared on the edge of the darkness just out of the light of the sun. Our eyes suddenly grew in shock when the two animals of different sizes stepped out and revealed themselves to us. A smirk quickly came upon our faces when we realized that the prisoners were none other than Briann and Trippe. They appeared dirty from the room and their eyes squinted, even Trippe's eyes whose eyes bounced around. Their faces glowed when they saw TC and me standing near the front door as if we had been some sort of dream.

"Is anyone going to break the silence?" asked the ant as he looked at all of us. I then looked down at him and then looked back up at my brother's old friends as they stood still in the light.

"So may I ask what crime they committed?" I asked the ant as TC stepped closer to his old friends.

"They are charged with butchering once funny puns into a thousand pieces," replied the ant.

"Yeah, apparently not everyone enjoys my comedic flare," said Trippe as Briann climbed up his tail and then stood on top of his back.

"I bet that is a total surprise," said Briann. TC and I looked at each other with a smirk as Trippe's sight turned to Briann.

"Was that some hamster sarcasm I sensed out of you?" replied Trippe.

"Certainly was, you crazy creature you," said Briann as she quickly jumped off his back before Trippe could smack her with his tongue.

"So how long is their punishment?" asked TC. The ant looked at TC and then at the two of them until he finally looked back at TC.

"Until they can apologize for destroying comedy," said the ant as we turned to Trippe.

"I will do it when pigs fly and believe me, my friend cannot fly," said Trippe as TC walked over to the side of him.

"You won't apologize?" asked TC as Trippe's eyes turned towards him.

"I will do no such thing," replied Trippe when suddenly TC took his claw and smacked Trippe in between his eyes.

"Apologize, you stubborn cold-blooded comedian," demanded TC as Trippe used his tongue to wipe the tears from his eyes.

"Fine, I'm sorry for crushing comedy like a bug," said Trippe.

"Not how I would have worded it, but it will set you free," replied the ant as he walked out of the door. Just as he reached outside, Bucky reappeared outside the doorway and looked outside.

"Hey, I need you upstairs immediately," said Bucky as he pointed in my direction.

"Enjoy your freedom guys," I replied as I hopped over to Bucky.

Just as I reached Bucky, he hopped over to the brightened doorway that was clear thanks to TC's massive claws. I watched as we passed through the doorway as the webdoor spider had begun the repair to the webdoor. We passed through the main room and then headed upstairs toward an opened door. Once inside of the room, I found myself in a room covered in newspaper that held a window in the shape of a carrot. I stopped in the middle of the room as Bucky headed towards the window. He turned his head outward to stare at the starry sky, which appeared to contain a billowed smoke.

"It appears that tomorrow will be the day that you have waiting for," said Bucky as he continued to face outside.

"What do you mean?" I asked.

"That was dumb, he clearly means the day you take down Saucy," said a voice to my left. I looked over and once again in my sight appeared Lio's spirit but this time he was not as visible as before.

"Why can't I see you as clearly?" I asked him as he looked down upon his arms.

"I guess you have just about figured out that you are stronger than you had ever given yourself credit for," replied his spirit as he looked back up before he disappeared out the window.

"I mean the day that you will head to your fate," said Bucky as he turned his head back to me.

"How can you tell?" I asked, uncertain about what exactly made the next day so special.

"That's simple, tomorrow is the day your brother was killed," replied a voice from behind me. I quickly looked behind me to find Master Tarroc slowly making his way into the room. He made his way towards Bucky as my eyes followed even if my mind stood in wonder.

"I almost had to tell him," said Bucky as Master Tarroc looked outside of the window.

"Yeah, especially since you are the leader here why would you need more responsibility," replied Master Tarroc as he turned to me.

"You read my mind," said Bucky with a smile as Master Tarroc quickly glanced back at him.

"I was using rabbit sarcasm but apparently you didn't catch it," said Master Tarroc.

"Not to interrupt but can I go and figure out a plan?" I asked as I began to turn around towards the door.

"Ok Pakul, take care," replied Master Tarroc as I began to walk out the door.

As I walked out of the doorway, I could hear the two rabbits behind me as they bickered about responsibility. I quickly laughed them off as I hopped downstairs to find myself faced with my brother's spirit on the bottom stair. The room appeared bare as my brother stood alone as he floated by the bottom stair. He stood in silence as I continued to make my down towards him until I stopped just a stair shy of his floating body.

"I will get him for you," I said to him.

His spirit looked me up in the face and then nodded his head before he disappeared as things returned to normal. The furniture in the room returned along with the others who stood in the main room. As I saw no one that I thought looked familiar, I proceeded down and out of the building as I entered the main town. The town remained busy as the sun had crested just over the building that now stood behind me. As I admired the work being done around the town, I began to progress downward to the edge of town where I found myself face to face with a familiar person. It was Camiya and everything about her seemed different, as if the once innocent porcupine had been replaced by a more aggressive version. She stood talking to an ant while each arm lay on a quill that had been placed onto the ground. As I made my approach, she quickly looked back when my shadow covered the ant in darkness.

"Well hello there," said Camiya as the ant scurried away towards a nearby building.

"Hey, so I was wondering what happened to your running buddy Lamajo?" I asked as I continued to hop closer to her. Her face filled with disappointment as she stared down upon her arm.

"He felt that I was slowing his quest of greatness down so he ran off," replied Camiya as her face reddened in rage.

"Oh I'm sorry to hear. So how did you get involved with this here?" I asked her with the hopes it would lessen the anger in her face.

"Bucky came to my rescue when I stood face to face with a hungry fox," replied Camiya who breathed the anger away.

I nodded my head and watched as she pulled the two quills out of the ground and held the safe part in her hands. Before I could say anything more, suddenly a loud noise began to fill the air which sent all of the creatures towards the main entrance. As I stood unsure where to go, Camiya grabbed my hand and dragged me to the main entrance as Bucky rushed through the crowd.

"What is it?" asked Bucky upwards to the guard tower.

"Creatures on the edge of town," replied TC as he stood on the top of the guard tower looking over the line of brush.

"Friends or foxes?" asked Bucky as he made his way to the front of the group that stood in front of the snakeskin door.

"Appears to be of the rodent family," replied TC as Bucky raised his hands to the beetles as they pulled back the snakeskin.

Chapter 9

As the skin pulled away, through the brush I spotted the rodent that TC had talked about. The creature was brown and running toward us in a similar fashion as someone I had encountered earlier. Suddenly, Camiya pops her head out of the group with her eyes bugged out.

"Lamajo!" yelled Camiya as my eyes suddenly jumped back to the running rodent. He quickly rushed passed the brush and entered the town where Camiya met him with a tear in her eye.

"Why hello there," said Lamajo to Camiya as he walked over to Bucky.

"So what is the news?" asked Bucky as Camiya stood still as tears rolled off her nose and onto the floor.

Camiya watched on as Lamajo and Bucky headed away from the group towards the building where I had walked. Camiya then shook her head as the group dispersed back to business as the two walked just past me. They suddenly stopped when Lamajo spotted me just outside of the group. A smirk showed upon my face as my hand reached down to grab the radish chuck at my side.

"That's the purple rabbit hero," said Bucky as Lamajo continued to stare at me.

"Yeah, we go way back," replied Lamajo as he and Bucky continued past me towards the building.

I shook my head as I turned to see that Camiya had disappeared from my view as the group had almost completely evacuated back to normalcy. I watched as TC had the snakeskin door placed back upon the entrance of the town. My eyes quickly glanced at the sky, which had turned to an orange-reddish color with the approaching sunset. As my eyes wandered, I watched as all the people that I had met along the way since my brother was stewed had come into town. As quickly as the snakeskin door was put up, the night came up onto the sky above. Fireflies above lighting the sky placed the city in transition as things just about shut down. I headed back over to the building I had walked out of where in the doorway stood Master Tarroc with Bucky.

"Is everything all quiet?" I asked as I hopped closer to them. Master Tarroc turned to Bucky who nodded his head back in response to what appeared as a silent gesture.

"I am sorry to say but TC, Briann, and Trippe have not been accounted for," replied Bucky.

"How do you lose three of my friends?" I said angrily as hopped closer to Bucky.

"He didn't, they just up and left the town," said Master Tarroc as I calmed down a bit as Bucky relaxed against the bony doorframe.

"Oh, then my apologies to you Bucky," I replied as Bucky nodded his head once again as he hopped into the building followed by Master Tarroc.

As all of us made our way inside, we headed upwards to the room next to Bucky's office. Inside of the room were three grass and moss hammocks next to the open face of the building. I watched as Bucky grabbed his hammock, so I quickly claimed the one next to the edge of the window. Master Tarroc however stood there with a smirk as we made ourselves comfortable which was not easy with the blades of grass poking me in the back.

"Well good night and remember tomorrow is the big day," said Master Tarroc as he walked out of the room.

"Yeah, so sleep good 'cause you are going to be fighting for all of us," said Bucky as he hopped out of his hammock.

"What you up to? I asked as I turned to watch as he tried to hop out of the room.

"Its official town-leading business," he replied as he hopped out of the door. As I continued to lie in bed, I shrugged and closed my eyes with the thoughts about just what exactly tomorrow was going to bring me.

The night came and went as uneventful as my life had been before this adventure began as my eyes opened to the sun. Its rays of light exploded through the window that stood next to me as I tried to ignore the shine. Just as I was about to try to go back to sleep, the thoughts of how today was truly the day where I would get my revenge for my brother.

"My soul will be with you in this fight against Señor Saucy," said a voice as I opened my eyes. Once again, my brother's soul had appeared as it stood at the edge of my hammock. I hopped out of the hammock and wiped my eyes as his spirit jumped on top of the hammock.

"I thought you were gone for good," I replied as he began to hop up and down upon the hammock which didn't move, but for how high he jumped, you could swear it was.

"Nope that wouldn't be any kind of brotherly love," he replied as he jumped off the hammock and onto the floor next to my feet.

"So what's the plan then?" I asked when suddenly my brother's spirit faded once again.

"Who are you talking too?" asked a voice from behind me. I turned around to find Bucky standing next to Lamajo in the doorway.

"I was talking to myself and what is he doing here?" I said back as I looked over at Lamajo whose eyes dropped downward.

"He came to apologize," replied Bucky as he shoved Lamajo towards my direction.

"Yeah I feel really bad about leaving you back there," said Lamajo as I turned around and grabbed a hold of my radish chucks as I placed them back upon my sides.

"Do you accept it?" asked Bucky as I turned around to find Lamajo still standing where I had left him when I turned my eyes away.

"Yeah, it was no big deal, besides I kicked his butt earlier that day," I replied with a bit of a chuckle. Bucky turned towards Lamajo who shook his head with a bit of a smirk peeking from the disappointed face.

"Okay, well do you plan to say farewell to your friends?" asked Bucky as Lamajo stepped back towards him and then walked out of the room.

"Yeah, I guess it would be the right thing to do in case I don't come back," I replied.

"Well then I guess I should tell you that it seems that we have lost Camiya, your mantis friend and the hamster," replied Bucky as Lamajo turned around swiftly.

"What do you mean lost?" asked Lamajo as he stopped in the hallway.

"As in they are no longer in town and we don't know where they went," replied Bucky. Lamajo's jaw dropped as he quickly rushed down the stairs and out of my sight as Bucky turned back to me.

"What about the chameleon?" I asked as I stepped closer to Bucky in the doorway.

"Them too, but they were seen heading in the direction of the fox hole," replied Bucky.

Without saying a word, I quickly hopped past him and down the stairs as I zipped past the creatures in the main room. As I exploded out of the building, I rushed towards the main gate when suddenly I spotted a familiar face awaiting me in front of it. It was Lamajo who I thought had gone after Camiya. I suddenly stopped just in front of him as tears began to drop off the sides of rodent cheeks.

"He is right, she is gone," said Lamajo as he wiped his face clear of the tears.

Before I could respond, he ripped back the gate and rushed back out into the brush that surrounded the town. As I watched him disappear into the thick green, my mind filled with the thoughts of taking down Señor Saucy. My head nodded and I rushed out behind him as I dodged all the rogue branches that blocked the path. Once I got past the original line of brush, I found myself alone on a plain with no idea about which direction I needed to go.

Indeed, I once knew but the scenery had changed and now I stood alone as I turned all about trying to find my former home. Then the thoughts exploded in my head about whether or not my family was still alive or more importantly if they would even recognize me. I mean it has been a long time, and a lot has happened since we left that troubled night, and I am a different color.

As my eyes bounced back and forth, suddenly my ears caught a sound from the distance that was out of the ordinary. I looked downward to find that my feet stood upon a makeshift road and the pebbles were vibrating. The noise grew louder when my eyes caught the sight of a creature running towards my direction. I quickly hopped off the road and landed in the weeds that lined the road. The creature slowed and then stopped directly where I had stood as it tried to catch its breath. The creature was a bit larger than I was when I began to examine the creature with the belief that I had seen it before. Then it struck me, this creature was the one outside of the rock inside of Tortabbi. I quickly tried to put together a plan to get the information I want from it.

"I'll just do what I always do," I whispered to myself as I grabbed hold of my radish chucks. I yelled as I hopped out of the weeds and began to charge at the creature that stood frozen on the road. I swung my radishes to no avail, in fact it seemed like I was not even hurting the creature at all.

"What are you hoping to accomplish?" the creature said as it brushed me off which sent me off into the weeds again.

"I want to find out how to get to Hareville," I replied as I rose up and hopped onto the creature's back.

"No one calls it Hareville anymore," said the creature as it tried to shake me off its back.

"I don't care, I need to go there to defeat the foxes," I said as I hopped off its back and quickly smacked the creature in the face before I landed in front of it.

"Ouch, I'll tell you just put those things away," the creature replied as I hesitantly lowered my radish chucks. It then tried to look down at the mark I left as I stood in front as I awaited his response.

"So where is it?" I asked as I grabbed hold of my radish chucks once again.

"Where is what?" replied the creature as it stared back down to me,

"Hareville," I said angrily as tightened my grip on my weapons.

"I don't know of this place but there is a fox hold just down this road," replied the creature. As I let go of my weapons, I watched as the creature shook off the blow and began to move down the road.

"Hey wait a second, what's your name?" I asked the creature as it turned its head towards me.

"I'm not really sure, but they call me Dilla," replied the creature as he took a couple of steps past me.

"Alrighty Dilla, thank you for the help I'm off to that fox hold," I replied as Dilla began to hasten his pace down the road.

I then watched as after a few steps, he suddenly began to run off down the road towards where he had pointed. After a few seconds, I then saw no trace of him and was once again all alone uncertain about what awaited me. However, what I knew was that what awaited me was the very thing I needed to get my revenge. Señor Saucy was there, I was sure of that, and I did not care the odds, I was going to exact some revenge.

I began to hop down the road behind Dilla and wherever he had gone. As my feet moved on the road, the sun moved above in the sky as the time passed as the distance between me and the town grew smaller. I suddenly stopped when I spotted a lone tree along the hillside just off my side. I looked up to the sky and felt the blazing heat on my fur as the sun had arrived directly above me.

My tongue had dried and ears had moistened as my body's temperature had risen from the lack of coverage around me. I quickly hopped towards the soft grass and the tree as I changed my plans to make my move during a shadier time of day. The grass provided a cooler ground than the rocky road as I made my way towards the tree and its full set of foliage. I looked ahead as I saw the tree as it surrounded by a circle of shade, which appeared to have been drawn into the grass beneath it. As I drew closer to it, the relief of a cooler shade began to set in over the burning of my skin from the intense heat above. I stepped into the ring of shade and instantly felt relief from the heat as the leaves covered the area. As I examined this trunk, I found it to be different from the one Master Tarroc was in since it had no hole. After I had looked around, I sat with my tail against the trunk as I waited for the sun to drop a bit. My thoughts ran away as I wondered if I was wasting time and what exactly I was going to find when I got there.

"Enough!" I yelled out as my way of quieting the thoughts as the silence regained control of my surroundings.

I watched as the grass waved and the clouds moved in the sky as if to allow the sun to have a clear path. After some time had passed, I got up from the ground and once again grabbed hold of my radish chucks as I prepared to leave. With a deep breath, I hopped away from the trunk back towards the road that I had left. The heat seemed less bothersome since I left it earlier, which made my feet happier when they dropped onto the rocky path. As I cleared the last bit of grass, my eyes laid on the road as I blanked on which direction I had to go. I looked both ways as I tried to remember, when I looked down and spotted the familiar tracks of that creature who had given me directions in the first place.

With a swift nod, I began to hop in the direction that he had pointed me in as I found myself newly motivated. I was not just doing this for me, but for those people in New Hareville who were forced to run from the foxes. Thoughts of my brother came into mind, which caused my hops to increase in stride. As I hopped through the territory, it was no different as the miles I had gone just simply being grass with an occasional tree or shrub. My breath began to deepen which caused me to stop when I heard a familiar sound. It was that berry-loving Monty, who was now charging the path from behind me. His eyes were wide as his beak stood open which allowed his tongue to hang to his chin as he sped in my direction. His tail fluttered as he stopped next to me to my pleasure since he would have clearly left me flat.

"You're quite the roadrunner," I said to him as his body swelled as he took in air.

"Hey wait, aren't you that rabbit I thought was food?" asked Monty as his head slowly leaned to one side.

"That's me," I answered as I wiped the dust from my face.

"I found you, I finally found you," said Monty as he began to jump up and down.

"What did you need to find me for?" I asked.

"I was sent to help make your trip easier by some old rabbit," replied Monty.

"How do you plan to do that?" I asked him.

"With this," he replied as he motioned to the cardboard lid wrapped around his stomach by a line of weeds. I walked over and bit through the line, which caused the cardboard to drop to the floor. I then knelt down and pulled it from his stomach out into the sun when I looked back up at him.

"What's this for?" I asked him as I continued to look at the lid.

"Put it behind my tail and then wrap the vine around my chest," replied Monty. I shrugged as I pushed the cardboard behind him and then grabbed the vine and wrapped it around its chest.

"Okay, what else?" I replied.

"Now tightly hold on to the vine and try to stay on the cardboard," replied Monty as I grabbed onto the vine.

As I held on, I got on top of the cardboard, unsure how this was going to allow me to go faster. Then before that thought could even finish developing, Monty exploded into a mighty sprint, taking me for a massive ride. As he ran, my hands nearly lost grip as the grass to my sides blew past me with amazing speed. The cardboard kept jumping up and down as I tried to keep my weight down so I would not fly off into the sky. As I began to get somewhat comfortable on it, I spotted the outskirts of the town I once called home. Monty began to slow down and then came to a stop just before the foxes at the guard post could see us. As I tried to regain my composure, I forced my hands open so I could drop the vine onto the floor. My feet shook as I raised one up so I could step off the box and back onto the dirt path. Once I was back on the path, I quickly regained my breath as Monty looked at me with a smirk on his beak.

"What's so funny?" I asked as I tried to look tough.

"You look funny," Monty replied as I realized what he was talking about. My fur looked like I had been shocked with it facing in one direction.

"Yes, well thanks for the ride," I replied as I tried to shake my fur straight.

"FOOD!" Monty yelled when he suddenly ran off the road through the grass as he left me alone.

"Well goodbye to you, too," I said aloud as I turned my attention to the guards who stood at the city's edge.

I watched as the two guards paced back and forth as I debated how exactly I planned to get by them. Then it hit me, I should use the surroundings to my advantage when it comes down to battle. I grabbed hold of the radish chucks and was about to hop towards them when suddenly the two guards doubled up. Two more guards rushed in with their hands waving, which forced me to rethink my original plan. As I stayed still, I watched as the four gathered up and then to my delight took off away from the entrance.

"I wonder if they are going after Monty," I thought to myself as I loosened my grip on my weapons.

I shrugged and hopped towards the vacant guard post as I had regained my focus. In what felt like the longest hops of my young life, I quickly found myself next to the guard post with not a fox in sight. I carefully hopped my way into the city, where I found that nothing had changed since the last time I had hopped through. It was still in ruins with broken windows and toppled doors all around the town. It was obvious I hadn't been spotted, since there was no sign of a fox anywhere around me. In fact, if it wasn't for the fact I had just seen them, I would have been certain I was completely alone.

I quickly shook off my thoughts as I turned my attention towards the direction of the Carrotminium that I had spent my youth in. As I made my way down that familiar alley, sudden sadness took over when I found myself face to face with the place I once called home. It was destroyed, the doorway laid clear and the windows broken as the glass laid on the grass outside. I hopped further into the building when I spotted the fallen door with a large

X that had been smeared from side to side. With a deep breath, I hopped into the house where everything had been destroyed with nothing left. As a tear began to roll down my puffy cheeks, suddenly a shadow appeared in the sunlight behind me. I quickly turned to find myself face to face with the armadillo that had helped me earlier, except this time he looked different.

"Sorry, but I must destroy you," it said when its head disappeared from my view and then suddenly it came crashing through the wall.

As shards of carrot flew, the house shook as the armadillo shook off the impact as I looked on in shock. It turned towards me with an evil gleam as it suddenly ran at me as I stood still. Before the armadillo hit me, I jumped out of the way onto the floor near where the door laid. The armadillo went crashing through the other side of the house, leaving a hole which shook the house violently. As I covered my head from the falling carrot pieces, the armadillo returned into the remains of the room even angrier.

"Why are you doing this?" I yelled over the carrots crashing onto the floor.

"Señor Saucy demands it," it said back with an evil smirk.

Just as it was about to charge at me again, the house's foundation began to give away all around the room. We both looked around in shock when suddenly it turned and ran toward me once again. It managed to dodge all the falling debris, crashing through the doorway and left me inside. The roof began to crumble as my thoughts contemplated my demise, when from out of one of the holes in the side stood my brother's spirit. My eyes went dark as the loud crashes got worse as the pieces grew in size. After a while the crashing stopped, and I opened my eyes to find myself unscathed except for a cut on my shoulder. Somehow, I had managed to make it outside before the building crashed down upon me. I turned around to find the house destroyed and no sign of the armadillo that had attacked me. As I continued to wonder how I had survived, I look around at my surroundings for any sign of life. Blood dripped from my fur and I found my radish chucks still intact at my feet.

"Get him," whispered the wind as I bent down with my injured arm to grab hold of the radish chuck.

I grimaced as I rose up with the weapon hanging from my hand with a new sense of confidence. Maybe after all this I do have the power and confidence that I had always seen inside of my brother.

As I took a deep breathe, I spotted a fox running in the middle of the area where the market was once. He looked both ways, for what I wasn't sure, and then bent down to knock on something and he suddenly disappeared through the floor. My eyes widened as I hobbled over to where I had seen the fox disappear from my sight.

Below my feet, laid a wooden door which was installed into the ground, for what I wasn't sure but I was going to find out. I reached for the knob to find it tight and unable to move. I knocked on the door when it suddenly dropped open, which caused me to fall through. The fall was no big deal as I landed in an underground tunnel of some sort. As I examined all around, I found myself surrounded by dirt except for a tunnel opening directly in front of me. I grasped tightly onto my radish chuck as I made my way forward through the tunnel. As each inch passed, I could feel as things got tighter and darker as if I had not made any progress. The silence had engulfed me and the little light I had was provided by the carrot torches that stood upon the walls which allowed me to see somewhat of where I was going.

After a few steps more, I found myself upon an open lit room which was much larger than the tunnel I had left. I stepped inside, where to my shock I found the old rabbit market sitting underneath the very town it once stood in. I examined it to see that its roof had just leveled with the rest of the ground, thus not showing any difference in the town above. I then found another tunnel opening on the opposite end of the tunnel which seemed to lead to a pathway. Before I could step further into the room, the door of the market crashed down as from underneath appeared two moles. The moles shook off the dirt as they turned to each other in the doorway.

"Just admit I'm faster, Max," said the other mole. The mole who I'm assuming was Max turned to the other with a smile upon his mole face.

"Please, you're lucky, not faster, Elom," replied Max as he stepped in front of Elom.

"What's that look for?" asked Elom as I continued to look on from the shadowy tunnel. Max pointed at the broken doorframe which caused Elom to turn around.

"We best not tell Master about this, otherwise he'll be mad because he didn't do it himself," said Max. I began to grow madder when I began to think he was clearly talking about Señor Saucy.

"Oh, well if he asks, we'll just say he did it and he just doesn't remember doing it," replied Elom.

"Ask about what," said a voice from the shadow tunnel on the opposite side.

As my eyes tried to see who it was, they exploded when Señor Saucy himself stepped out from the shadows with two foxes in tow. My legs nearly buckled as the anger began to take over as I watched him as he approached the two moles.

"Nothing sir, we were just improving our speed," said Elom as he quickly kicked a fragment of the frame out of his sight. One of the foxes began to point to something as he whispered something into the ear of Señor Saucy. Saucy then took a couple of steps to the side and nodded his head when he spotted whatever he was looking for.

"What happened to the door frame?" asked Señor Saucy as the moles turned to one another.

"Your master asked a question, foolish mole!" yelled one of the foxes behind Saucy.

"Calm down, Rode," replied Señor Saucy as the moles shook the sweat from beneath their eyes.

"Well you see master, your darn armadillo came through here and destroyed it," said Max as Elom nodded his head in agreement.

"That's interesting, especially since he is above ground taking care of an unwanted pest," said Señor Saucy as I looked at my shoulder and the dried blood on my fur.

The two foxes chuckled at the moles as they realized he had seen through the lie that.

"We are sorry sir, we were racing, and it fell when we reappeared," replied Elom as the foxes quieted their chuckle. Señor Saucy stood there in a silence when suddenly a sly smirk appeared on his face.

"That's nothing to lie about, besides I'm sure the market keeper won't mind in the foxhole," said Señor Saucy with a chuckle. He then made his way toward the broken frame as the other foxes stood by the opening to the tunnel where they had appeared from. He then walked between the two moles into the market where he found the pile of rubble.

"Rode, if you will," said Saucy as the two moles looked back to Rode who began to walk down along the wall. I watched as he stopped along the wall and suddenly jammed his foxy hand into the wall which shocked the moles.

"No, you said it was ok," said Elom. Just as he finished the last word, they suddenly fell through the ground into a cloud of orange smoke. The cloud suddenly vanished as quickly as it appeared, and Rode began to walk towards Señor Saucy.

"They should know better than to destroy anything without my approval," said Señor Saucy as the two foxes arrived at the outside of the market.

"Moles are so stupid," replied Rode as they stepped inside of the market.

"Indeed, I mean I wouldn't want anyone to discover the hidden entrance to the Foxhole," replied Señor Saucy.

"A hidden entrance?" asked the fox at Rode's side.

"Yes, Monta, to allow for an easy escape in case you know who tries to intrude," replied Rode.

"Who is that?" asked Monta.

"Please, Rode, hit him," replied Saucy as he placed his hand onto his head.

Rode then turned and slapped the back of Monta's head as Saucy stepped deeper into the market out of my view. Monta and Rode followed him inside when I suddenly lost any sense of them as if they had disappeared into thin air.

"Are they gone?" I asked myself as I slowly made my way inside of the room towards the market. As I cautiously made my way, I continued to hear nothing as I got closer to the building's frame. I stood up on the side of the wall next to where the opening of the doorframe was as I tried to gather up the courage to face this monster. With a mighty deep breath, I hopped into the doorway as my hands held the radish chucks tightly.

PAKUL

Chapter 10

As I dropped below the surface, my fur nearly dropped off my skin when I suddenly crashed into murky water. I quickly kicked myself back up to the surface where I found myself staring down the hole in which I had fallen. My eyes quickly shifted all around until I found the dry land my heart had desired since I landed in this water. As fast as I could, I kicked my feet as I slowly managed to get myself closer to the edge of the water.

However, instead of finding myself upon dirty land, I found myself on top a ground of shiny flakes that I had never seen before. As my feet touched down, the floor crunched as it gave a bit. After I shook off my fur, I gathered up my radish chucks and proceeded down the pathway deeper into this underground world. Before I could get any farther than a few feet, my ears picked up something that caused me to turn around.

However, when I turned, I found nothing out of the ordinary so I shrugged it off and continued forward toward this orange light at the end of the tunnel. My thoughts had turned to Saucy and his gang, when suddenly something whistled past my ear and smacked against the dirt above me. I quickly jumped around with my radish chucks in hand, only to find empty space all around me.

"Must have been my imagination," I said aloud as I relaxed my grip on my radish chucks. Before I could turn around, suddenly something brown jumped out of the water onto the ground in front of me. It stood tall and looked at me as if I was an enemy, which caused me to tighten my grip on my weapon.

"You are trespassing, seeing as you are no friend of Saucy," said the creature.

"Oh? And how do you know that?" I replied to it as I stood my ground.

"Simple. you didn't catch your fish scale badge," said the creature as it pointed down to the ground. My eyes lowered to find two unique scales on the multi-colored floor.

"I have no time for games, only revenge so goodbye," I said as I began to turn back around to try to leave the creature behind. Before I could turn around, I found myself once again face to face with the creature. It smirked as I peeked backwards to see that indeed it was the same creature that I had just left behind me.

"You're right, no games. Which means you will lose," said the animal as its sharp claws directed themselves at me.

"Says who?" I asked, unimpressed.

"Pez Cado is the name and taking you down is my game," he replied as he began to quickly sprint towards me. Before I could react, he jumped and soared between my ears, sharp pain shaking my body.

"You're going to pay for that," I said as some of the hairs from my ears fell towards the floor.

Pez rolled to his feet as he dropped the clump of hairs he had ripped from my ears into the murky water in front of him. He turned and tried the same move again, except this time I dropped my weapon to the ground and grabbed his body, stopping him in mid-air. However, my success was short lived, because Pez slipped out of my hand and landed back on his feet once again behind me.

"Rabbits have big ears and otters have slick skin," said Pez as he charged at me again.

This time he began to slide between my feet and before I could grab him, he had gotten past me, my radish chucks in his mouth. I watched as he smirked and jumped back into the water with my weapon still in his control. My anger rose as the water settled calmly onto its surface and the realization that this was not going to be easy began to hit me.

"You are going to pay for making me go into water!" I yelled as I hesitantly hopped into the water.

When I opened my eyes to the deep blue world, I found Pez staring at me with my weapon floating in his hand. With a smirk, he disappeared behind a burst of bubbles as he swam away. As the bubbles faded away, there was no sign left of him until I spotted a swift shadow moving back and forth in the water. I rose to the surface to catch a breath, but I was suddenly dragged back down as something grabbed on my foot. I looked downward and found Pez with both hands around my ankle as he continued to swim downward to the scaly bottom. Before he could drag me further, I managed to use my free foot to kick his hands and break free, once again heading for the surface. As my head broke the surface, I quickly spotted my radish chucks floating along the ripples of the water. My eyes widened as I quickly swam to the shore before he could catch me again.

"Where do you think you're going, rabbit?" asked Pez as he swam after me, just as my feet touched the scaly edge of the water. I smirked as I launched myself off the ground and over Pez's head, grabbing hold of my weapon. I rose back to the surface with my weapon in hand as Pez looked back at me in disbelief.

"I was going for all tens," I replied as I lifted my weapon out of the water.

Pez snarled as he quickly dove under the water as he headed towards me as I attempted to figure out my next move. Then suddenly above me, I spotted a piece of the wooden frame hanging just low enough for my ears to reach it. I managed to throw one end of the radish over it as I placed one hand onto each end. As my muscles tightened, I managed to lift myself out of the water as I hung by the radishes above the surface. Just as I exhaled, Pez reappeared on the surface as he looked all around for me.

"You're no rabbit, you're a furry chicken," he chuckled.

"Nope, just half brain coral," I said as Pez looked upward. I dropped onto Pez, who tried to quickly dive.

However, my feet smashed into his back as the wave of water sent him onto the coastline, out of air. As the shockwave dispersed, Pez remained face down on the scaly ground with two footprints on the fur of his back. I grabbed my radish chuck as I headed back to the shoreline where Pez laid unconscious. After I made it safely, I looked down with a smirk and shook myself dry as I faced once again the open pathway towards my true enemy. I began to walk the path, knowing that this was one thing I had to do for all of those I had met on this path. As I reached the open doorway, the familiar voices of Saucy and the other foxes filled my ears. Before I could step forward, a sudden gust chilled my fur as my brother's spirit appeared out of the wall next to me.

"You truly have grown since you fell into the mud when you tried to beat me," said the spirit with a smirk.

"Yes, well I'm doing this for all the rabbits who have been tortured by this evil fox," I replied as my eyes turned towards him.

"Just don't lose you in all this, because Brother you're not me," he replied as he faded away into the air once again.

The thoughts began to wonder in my mind, what did he mean by that and had I become worse than him in this whole experience? I quickly shook it off when I spotted the foxes making a move in my direction. I quickly jumped behind a beam of wood near where my brother's spirit appeared as I looked through a hole behind the beam. As I looked, Saucy was leading the other foxes towards my direction when they turned to a new direction and walked back into the middle of the room. Before I was going to make any moves, I decided to look around at this giant room, which held a throne which appeared to be made out of some kind of fur. The room appeared empty with nothing else besides the three foxes making their way towards the throne. As I continued, Señor Saucy approached the throne and sat down as he pointed to the sky as the other two quickly ran to opposite ends of the room. The other foxes grabbed hold of some kind of rope and pulled, causing the entire underground to shake as a chunk of the roof dropped out of the center. I quickly made my move. I hopped from behind the beam into the view of the room when suddenly Saucy spotted me as he rose from his throne.

"Well, what do we have here?" said Saucy as the other two stopped what they were doing.

"What about the others?" replied Rode who stood at the other end of the room.

"They can wait. We have an almighty hero in our midst, boys," said Saucy mockingly as I took a step into the room.

"Saucy, what have you done to the rabbits of this town?" I yelled. Saucy turned to Monta and Rode who then began to chuckle in unison.

"You foolish rabbit, I have done nothing but sent them to work. Well, at least the strong," replied Saucy.

"How about the others?" I asked as my hand gripped tighter onto the radish chucks.

"Braised in a nice carrot bath just like your brother," replied Monta who released his rope, which sent the chunk of the roof back upwards.

"Oh, did you think we wouldn't recognize a rabbit who managed to escape thanks to an Aquarrot?" replied Señor Saucy as he crossed his leg over as he sat back on the throne.

"Enough words. This is for my brother!" I yelled as I began to charge the head fox when suddenly Rode and Monta pulled once again on the rope, bringing down the large chunk of the roof. As the chunk fell from the top, five foxes fell from the chunk and onto the ground just as the chunk settled. To my surprise, I noticed some familiar faces on the top of the chunk. It was Master Tarroc and all my friends who stepped off as Señor Saucy's jaw dropped as he stood in front of his throne.

"Isn't this a twist of a branch," said Señor Saucy as the other foxes quickly ran over to him.

As I joined up with my allies who stood behind me, Saucy turned to Monta and Rode who simply snapped their fingers. The ground shook as the wall that had stood behind them had now dropped to reveal a fox squad of fighters. Amongst the army of foxes was the armadillo that attacked me earlier, except it was all chained up under the control of the army.

"What's wrong? Do you recognize your friend there, hero?" asked Señor Saucy as his army gathered around him.

"Who is it?" whispered TC as he stepped a bit closer to me.

"It helped Lio and me before Lio was … you know," I replied.

"He means broiled!" yelled Saucy as he chuckled.

"So which of you hams care to make the first move?" said Trippe.

"Trippe, you realize they are foxes not pigs right?" asked TC as he turned his head back to Trippe who just nodded his head.

"What just bit me?" said Saucy as he reached to his shoulder and lifted up a familiar hamster. Saucy snarled as he threw Briann over our heads as the foxes chuckled. Trippe spit out his tongue and grabbed hold of Briann as he brought her in to safety.

"Sneak attack," squeaked Briann as the foxes when silent.

"What are you doing here? Attack, my army!" yelled Señor Saucy as suddenly the army of foxes began to charge at me and my allies.

"Get them!" I yelled as my allies charge them and began to engage the foxes into battle.

However, we suddenly stopped when the front line of foxes was taken out by Camiya, who had snuck in and tackled her way through the room. After a second or two, the foxes continued the fight, as did we. Two rogue foxes had rushed into a fight with me but before they could get a paw on me, I quickly dispatched them by simple jamming my radish chucks into their chests. As they lay prone on the ground, I turned to watch as Señor Saucy began to try to run through to the back room to avoid any danger. I quickly rushed towards him by stepping on one of the foxes, who groaned as my big foot hit his back. As I managed to avoid any battles to reach the back of the room, suddenly I was a direct path away from Saucy himself.

"No more running, you cowardly fox!" I yelled out above the battling behind me.

Before Saucy could respond, a fox was suddenly launched into the wall when the armadillo managed to break away from the handlers which had held him down. The armadillo shook off the others as it managed to run in between Saucy and myself. As my hands gripped my weapons tighter, the armadillo quickly turned around at Señor Saucy who then ran towards the stairs.

The armadillo began to chase him and would have gotten him if it wasn't for the tight area of the stairs which allowed him to get away from it. As the armadillo stood staring at the stairway, I rushed forward and cut in front of the armadillo, charging forward at the fox that had caused all my pain. He stood at the top with his claws out as I raised my weapons to face him. Just as I reached him, his claws blocked my weapons as they became entangled at the very top of the stairs.

"Foolish like your brother," said Saucy as he gained the advantage as I dropped to my knee.

"Courageous like him too," I replied as I rose up and slammed him into the dirt wall.

He shook his head as he tried to break free by stepping on my toe and then spitting dirt in my face. As I tried to wipe it from my face, he swiped my face and chest with his claws as I dropped to a knee.

"That's right, beg me," he replied, when suddenly the stairs gave away to reveal a deep pit.

A smell began to fill my nose of something familiar when I caught a peek of the very orange liquid that had claimed my brother's life. I charged forward and tackled Saucy down to the ground, jumping to my feet. I began to walk towards him as my radishes hung to my side as he watched me grow closer to him. Suddenly from behind, a fox lunged towards me, however I dodged the attack and watched as it screamed as it fell into the pit of liquid. Before I could turn back, a pain hit the back of my head as I reached back to find a patch of fur missing. I turned around to find a glaze-eyed Señor Saucy as my blood dripped from his mouth. He went for another bite, except this time, I sent him into the wall with a radish haymaker. As he struggled to get up, I grabbed him by the scruff of his neck as I pulled off his eye patch and then threw it down.

"I'm going to send you down like the fox you are," I said as I shoved him into the wall repeatedly in order to break him down. As he struggled to stand, I let go of his scruff and then tossed him down towards the edge of the ground. As I turned towards him, I suddenly noticed Master Tarroc at the other side of the pit.

I then looked down to find that the amulet had returned to the fur around my neck, but before I could make a move, Señor Saucy tried to grab hold of me but I kicked him off. Not realizing my strength, he landed at before Master Tarroc and missed the pit completely as I now stood alone at the opposite end of the pit. I then backed up a few steps and then ran forward up the edge of the pit when I hopped a mighty hop where I landed just barely on the other side. Master Tarroc and I both looked down upon at Saucy, who tried to get up by our legs. We then looked at one another before I gave a little kick, which knocked him back down.

"We did it," I said to him as I grabbed him Saucy's foot and began to drag him into view of the rest of my friends.

"No Pakul, you did it," replied Master Tarroc as he gave me a pat between my ears. We arrived into the view of the rest of my friends, whom stood bruised and battered but began to cheer. We made our way through the foxes that lay scattered on the floor as I dropped Saucy at the feet of my friends.

"The mighty Saucy is now our prisoner!" I yelled as my friends once again began to cheer loudly. This moment had haunted my dreams for a lifetime, except now I experienced a sense of relief. My allies circled around Saucy as he lay motionless on the ground while I stood in the back near the throne. Just as I was about to sit down upon it, suddenly the circle gasped as Saucy made his way through the group.

"I'm not down yet!" yelled Señor Saucy as he stumbled his way out of the circle.

"I knew that, I just wanted to see how long it took for you to rise to your sly feet," I replied as Saucy stopped for a second then fell back to a knee.

"That's right, you beg like the fox you are," said Lamajo from out of the circle. He then rose back up to his feet as he stumbled towards me as I twirled my radish chucks.

"Enough, you guys, this is in Lio's honor. Not a celebration to demean," I replied as I rose from the throne.

Before they could respond, Saucy tried for one final attack which grazed my shoulder fur as he crashed into the throne. The throne tumbled backward as it, along with Saucy fell backward near the edge of the orange pit. We watched as Saucy struggled to his feet as he used the throne for balance.

"I shall not go down to anyone's hands but my own!" he roared when he let go of the throne. Saucy fell backwards into the pit as we all watched in disbelief at what had occurred. After a second or two, the scream and his body had completely vanished from view. As we exhaled, a plume of orange smoke rose through the hole and then faded away. As I watched on, my brother's spirit reappeared, rising from the hole and waving to me as it went through the roof.

"Your brother would be proud," said TC as he placed his claw upon my shoulder.

"Yeah man, who would have known you'd become so tough," said Trippe as Briann placed herself upon his back.

"I had help," I replied as I turned around, followed by them.

One by one the entire group stepped upon the circle, which rose back up once we all stepped aboard. Once we got back to the top, the sun removed all of which had burdened us below. Then, as if we had seen the broken ruins of the town in a new light, a changed wind had swept through our minds.

"We can rebuild this," said TC as he broke the silence of the group.

"I think we should leave it and expand on what we have," replied Bucky as he tried to shake the dust from his fur.

"What do you think Pakul?" asked Master Tarroc as I stood, taking in the emptiness of the ruins of my former home. The question of what to do next had left me uncertain about where I should go and had me as confused as ever.

"I think you all should work on New Hareville, while I figure out what to do next on my own," I replied as I stepped toward the broken remains of one of the buildings.

"Are you sure?" asked Briann.

"Sadly, this is what is best," replied Master Tarroc before I could respond. I turned around and saw the sadness in their faces, even though I knew inside they all understood what I had said.

"Well Bucky, Camiya and I will meet you there," replied Lamajo as they began the trek to New Hareville.

"Wait for me," said the armadillo that lifted the two up as they continued down the dirt path.

"Well, I guess I have some plans to make up," replied Bucky as he saluted all of us and then went down the path in a sprint. This left Master Tarroc, Briann, TC, Trippe, and I standing next to the chunk of ground that had placed us back onto the surface.

"What about you guys?" I asked as they all stood silent as they looked at me.

"I'm going to find another spot away from everything, but don't worry. I will never be too far," said Master Tarroc as Monty showed up at his side. Master Tarroc jumped onto Monty as they took off in the opposite direction of the rest of the group. All that remained was my brother's former group along with me, and yet I feel they looked at me like they had my brother.

"I think I'm going to go back to New Hareville. They seem to need some brute strength to help them," said TC as he turned around.

"Take care of yourself and thank you for all of your help," I replied as Briann and Trippe followed him out of the town. As I watched them disappear at the horizon, the realization that I was now in the next phase of life had begun to hit me.

Well, that was my story and I how I found myself upon the porch of a building which is on the outskirts of the Hareville ruins. I sit here with the hopes that one day rabbits may return here to look at the memorial for the battle in which a so-called heroic rabbit took down an evil gang of foxes along with a group allies.

PAKUL